The publisher and author acknowledges the trademark status and trademark ownership of all trademarks, service marks, and word marks mentioned in this book.

Published by Sandra A. Sigfusson. This book is available in e-book, paperback and audiobook.

I0638641

Reader Reviews:

★★★★★I very much enjoyed the audio of this story! It was hot, steamy and sexy in all the right ways. One thing I really love about Sandra's writing is it isn't just the typical romance story where the climax builds, comes to a peak and then it's an HEA. Sandra throws in little twists and turns you don't expect and I love that! It adds so much more to the story and keeps you wondering what will happen next. I sat and listened to this straight through and enjoyed every minute of it. I'm an audio book lover and the audio version of this did not disappoint! Tim Paige and Ava Lucas brought the story to another level! They were perfect narrators for these characters. Highly recommend the audible version of The Art of Love! – Kristy Gleeson via Goodreads

★★★★Wow, Sandra gave us a lot in this book. What happens when one love burns out? Olivia is an artist who married her professor 19 years ago. A year ago Carl had a stroke, and he's changed. They have separate rooms now and they are little more than roommates.
Olivia expresses herself with her art, and with the people she's meeting through her art. Teddy and Max are both surprises in her life. She really goes on a journey to learn who she is and if she can love again. Very emotional journey for her, love and loss, exploration. It's all there. Very enjoyable listen with the audiobook. – KK via Goodreads

★★★★★Such a wonderful book! I listened to this book on Audible and I so love Ava Erickson the female narrator!
This is a fast-paced book with an amazing storyline. Olivia is finding herself after being married for so many years. She is an amazing artist; she paints and sculpts. Max a real estate agent loves her work When Max meets Olivia they have such a strong sexual attraction. And Olivia is enjoying herself, since she never

The Art of Love

in New York City

Sandra A. Sigfusson

The Art of Love in New York City
Copyright 2020 All Rights Reserved

Title: The Art of Love in New York City / Sandra A. Sigfusson

Description: Romance, Contemporary

Identifiers: ISBN: 978-1-989829-04-2

Subjects: Contemporary Romance – fiction | Interpersonal
Relationships – fiction | Contemporary Women – fiction | Art
Collecting – fiction | Artist – fiction | New York – fiction | Real Estate -
fiction | LGB - fiction

First Edition

Book Cover Design: Sandra A. Sigfusson

Cover Image: iStock.com / Deagreez - Stock photo ID:
936419850

iStock.com / Maica - Stock photo ID: 1030338298

Editor: Michael Dolan / Brooklyn, New York

had this with her husband. I was happy for Olivia as I listened to this book, it's filled with discovery and steamy love scenes and a great flowing story line. Love the narrative, the characters and the ending! Definitely going to listen to this book again =) - Sonia N. via Goodreads

Contents

Chapter 1 – Olivia

The second I heard the long, loud blast of a car horn, my heart nearly jumped out of my chest. A honking horn in New York City is as common as birds chirping in the forest, but this alarming blow was meant for me. The music in my earbuds sheltered me in my little world, and I hadn't noticed the car speeding around the corner at the same time my toes passed the curb and grazed the pavement of the street.

Leaping backward, I realized the honk was not only a warning but a signal to awaken. My thoughts are scattered, but for more reasons than this incident.

My hand raises to ensure the male driver that I'm fine, minus the heart palpitations, and the driver, shockingly, waves and smiles at me. Only in New York can someone who nearly killed with their impatience would still manage to find time to flirt with you afterward.

I end my morning run with a slower-paced jog as I near my favourite haunt for coffee and pastries. My t-shirt weighs heavily with sweat, and my breathing has become ragged. As I pause to catch my breath, I bend over and place my palms on my thighs to read the menu on the chalkboard outside the café's door. I decide on two Americano coffees and two lemon-filled Danishes for Carl and me to share.

When I return to the apartment, Carl is still resting in bed. Calling out his name from the kitchen rouses him, and I hear the tell-tale sound of his slippers shuffling across the hardwood floor as he enters the room. "Sit," I say, gesturing to the island bar stool. "I brought you your favourite coffee and pastry for breakfast." I slide the Danish over the counter, which I plated neatly for him, open a vanilla yogurt, and set it beside the Americano coffee.

Carl nods and offers a small smile at my gesture. "Did you sleep well?"

He takes a bite of the Danish, a spoonful of his yogurt, and nods at me again. I wish that he would use his words rather than nodding, but he isn't the same man he was before the stroke. His doctors warned me that Carl's personality might take some drastic turns after his recovery, and they were spot on with that diagnosis. I feel like I'm married to a completely different man, and I have no idea how to deal with this stranger in my life. I had hoped that after all this time, I'd see glimmers of who *my* Carl was returning, but I fear I've lost my Carl forever.

Memories of how handsome he was while he lectured in the auditorium during my senior year flood my mind. Every step confident, every glance of his distinctive green eyes upon his students, the tone of his voice – deep and clear with just a hint of gravel to it – his genuine smile on the rare occasion that one of us would make him laugh; all these small things combined into a tempting package to me. I doubt I was the only one who thought there was something special about him. His humor was deftly smattered throughout his lectures, and I loved the way his mind worked and how his teaching style appeared to command everyone's attention. So many other professors bored me to tears, but Professor Carl Aston had a gift.

I remember trying to capture his attention with my questions, face to face at the end of one of his best lectures. When I stood next to him, I felt a bit of a rush, yet I doubted he felt the same way. But when we met again, it was months after I had graduated. I stood behind him in the order line in the very same coffee shop I pick up his danishes and coffees while on my daily runs. We sat together, chatted easily, and that is when I knew he did have an attraction to me while I was in his class, but he held that secret close.

9

The Art of Love in New York City

My mother scolded me when I told her how old Carl was. *"You shouldn't be dating a man so much older than you, Olivia."* Our age difference was never a barrier to us. I loved his mind, his introspectiveness, his humor, and we made love with such ease that in my mind, no other could be a better match for me.

That same year, Carl decided to take a one-year sabbatical from lecturing to write his first book. I moved into his apartment three months after our first date, and I think he thought I'd hang out, be his muse while he penned his novel, and then leave his side when I grew bored. But I never felt the need to leave. I would paint and sculpt beside him in the living room while he toiled with his prose on an old oak desk that was once his father's. We both had creative minds but on such different scales. His words were his art; my hands and visions were mine.

God, how I miss those days. Nineteen years have passed, and for the most part, we were the perfect couple – envied by our friends, and even my mother got over her age difference concerns when she realized how perfect Carl and I were for each other.

Though I know that he and I are no longer that couple, the reality of our situation hits me like a sucker punch to the gut. If he would only open up and talk with me, I might find the man I fell in love with hiding in there somewhere. But he remains predominantly silent. Perhaps I am also a stranger to him now.

I press my marriage dilemma to the back of my mind while I become inspired to paint the rose garden at the front of the church that I passed two blocks down from the café to help distract me. The image I captured on my cell phone helps me remember the details of the one-hundred-year-old wrought iron fence that lines the sidewalk and how the roses hung among the black wrought iron pickets in a lackadaisical display of various pinks and soft yellows.

It is reminiscent of a traditional English garden, replete with Boston Ivy weaving its long tentacled vines that cling vicariously to the brick facade around the church's dark red arched wooden double doors.

I smile swiftly at Carl as he takes his last bite of the Danish and washes it down with a sip of hot coffee. "I'm going to have a quick shower before heading upstairs to my studio to paint. Are you good on your own for a few hours?"

Carl nods again. "Fine then. I'll come back down when it's nearing lunch and prepare whatever you are hungry for." I pause for a moment to gaze into Carl's eyes. Those beautiful green eyes always had a hold on me. I force back the urge to cry for myself, knowing those eyes now belong to someone else, someone I have yet to understand and relearn to love.

I grow tired of feeling sorry for myself and what the stroke did to Carl. We sleep in separate beds, speak rarely, and feel awkward in each other's presence. When I agreed to love and cherish him for better or for worse, until death do us part, I had never considered my current situation was remotely possible. And as his continued silence reminds me he's not the Carl I married, I have to ask myself if I should break my vows for that reason or continue as regularly scheduled in the hopes that he will return to me one day?

A thundering ache fills my chest while the sound of the shower water streaming down upon my heaving body drowns the sound of my sobbing. I cannot do this anymore. I have a life to lead; I'm still vibrant and just as alive as I was in my twenties. I'm never going to recover what I lost ten months ago. To me, my husband is dead. The man in my kitchen is a stranger with whom I have nothing in common with exception that I bear his last name. I spin my wedding rings around my left-hand finger nervously while my sobbing subsides.

If I take these rings off, will I feel guilty for pretending I'm no longer attached? Will it help me to move forward or force me to fall deeper into my guilt? I think the only way to find out is to take these rings off my finger and see if Carl notices I'm no longer wearing them. He was not wearing his wedding band this morning and hasn't worn it for the past few weeks. If he has abandoned our marriage, then perhaps so should I.

Chapter 2 – Olivia

Soft light filters inside through the south-facing window, enhancing the pallet of colours I chose for the English garden scene in front of the church. I've used some artistic license with the overall scene, not wanting to replicate it perfectly as many have before me. The St. Augustine Catholic church is a common subject for photographers, painters, and writers because of its tall, ornate spire and striking architecture. Many churches built in the same era were equally ornate, but St. Augustine stands out as the most favoured.

As I add the finishing touches to the painting, I hear Carl downstairs making noises as if he is rummaging through kitchen drawers. I glance at the clock on the wall above the door to my studio and note that it is five minutes before noon. He's hungry, or bored, or both, and I should attend to him.

After placing my brush inside the jar of water to rinse it, I quickly dry my hands and descend the stairs to the kitchen. Carl has decided to make himself French toast, and he seems to have it under control. He doesn't struggle with everyday tasks, which I am eternally grateful for. His lack of communication has become the critical barrier in our relationship.

"Can you add two slices of bread to the pan for me?" I ask as I sit at the kitchen island bar. Carl nods but doesn't look over to me.

"Thank you," I say, then rise to wash my hands and to set two plates and cutlery at the bar for us when the meal is ready to serve. Quietly, Carl hums a song I don't immediately recognize.

There it is. A glimmer of who he once was. Carl always hummed when he cooked, and my heart skips a beat with this realization that he is in there somewhere. My Carl.

13

The Art of Love in New York City

"What is the song you are humming called?" I ask as I sit back down at the island bar. A quick side glance tells me he is willing to engage me with more than a nod today.

"I don't know the name of it. I heard it being played outside my bedroom window this morning from a street performer on the sidewalk. It has stuck with me all day. Let me continue to hum, and maybe you'll recognize the tune."

"Yes, of course. I love that you are humming again." Carl doesn't smile or nod before he returns to humming the song. After about the first few bars of notes from his baritone voice, filling my ears and heart, the melody is recognizable.

"Let It Be, by The Beatles," I say brightly.

"Is that what it is?"

"Yes, I'm certain. One of your favourites. Don't you recall it as one that you often played on your guitar for me?"

He thinks for a minute while he flips the bread over on the pan and shuffles the pieces to fit perfectly within it. "Yes. I should try to play it." As Carl checks the French bread's doneness, I retrieve the butter dish and the maple syrup from the pantry.

"Will you want tea with your lunch, or should I put on a pot of coffee?" I ask.

Carl places two pieces of bread upon my plate before replying with, "I'll have tea, please."

This is the longest conversation we've had in quite some time. Could this be a tipping point in his recovery? My mind races in circles, looking for subjects I can bring up that may interest him in continuing to chat with me. He sits next to me at the counter, pats the top of my thigh with his hand twice, and then digs straight into his meal without another word. My heart pounds in my chest a little harder after his gentle touch. I want to grab his face, force him to look at me, and kiss the living hell out of him.

He has not touched me, incidentally or intentionally, in the time since his stroke. I'm dying to be touched, to be loved, to be given a ray of hope that I can have my Carl back. My words spill unceremoniously like a glass of milk knocked from the table. "Why haven't you kissed me? Do I not appeal to you any longer?"

Between chews of his latest bite, he replies. "Would a kiss make you stop fussing over me like I were a small child?"

I swallow hard. "You think I'm treating you like a child?"

"In some ways, yes. I'm not broken, Olivia. I'm just different."

"How do you know you are different?" I ask, speaking softly to keep the conversation from potentially escalating to a fight.

"I live with you, and I understand that we are husband and wife, but if this is what marriage is supposed to be like, I don't like it. I can't imagine that at one time in my life, before or after the stroke, that I'd marry a woman and live in what can essentially be considered a bubble. I have my job, and a safe place to live, money in my bank account, but I'm not certain what it is that you and I are doing. Were we always like this?"

My jaw clenches, and I have to remind myself to relax. "No, Carl. We were happily married, had sex regularly, entertained friends and family nearly every weekend, and enjoyed our lives together. Since your stroke, you have become disconnected, distant, cold. I'm still the same woman you married eighteen years ago. Correction, nineteen years ago, as it was our wedding anniversary last week, but I feared bringing the subject up with you since you find it so difficult to talk to me most days."

My tone has become snide. I cannot hold back my hatred for

what has become of us. And now I'm beginning to understand his silence. He cannot differentiate between what we were to each other and what we are now. And my patience to correct this situation has drawn thin. "Tell me what you want to do, Carl. Are you unhappy?"

A brief moment of silence fills the small space between our bodies. A chill runs down my spine. I look upward to the ceiling and rapidly blink while I attempt to refrain from letting the welling tears fall.

"Yes," (he mumbles.)

"Yes, what? Yes, you are unhappy?"

"I want a divorce, Olivia. I don't want to be married to you or anyone else. I want to be alone."

As the shock of his admission registers, I rise from the stool and slip out of the kitchen to escape to my studio. When I've reached the second-floor landing, I fling myself through the studio door and slam it shut behind me. Tears and my crushing cries echo within the empty space. I don't care if Carl can hear me sobbing like a grieving widow over her husband's casket. This is a death to me. My entire life has been upended since Carl's stroke, and now the only thing I hoped was salvageable, our marriage and love for each other, is officially gone.

It takes me nearly twenty minutes to collect myself enough to go back downstairs and address Carl's request for a divorce. I cannot do this dance with him any longer. And if he has given up on us, what choice do I have but to let him go. I never imagined I'd be single again at the age of forty-five. I never imagined a life without Carl.

Chapter 3 – Max

I glance up briefly from the empty cocktail glass my hand is wrapped around to catch a reflection in the bar's mirror of an old associate of mine. "Jason," I say as I spin around on my seat and reach to shake his hand.

"Max? What the hell, man? Good to see you again," Jason replies. As expected, his grip on my hand is firm to the point of nearing painful, but Jason always had a firm grip on everything, from his handshake to his career.

"What brings you in here tonight?" I ask.

"A buddy of mine is getting married in two weeks. We're planning his stag night with the rest of the groomsmen. You're welcome to join us if you're not here with someone," he says, gesturing with his thumb out toward the crew of men behind him. I glance at the guys he's dragged into the bar with him and grin.

"I'll take a raincheck on the invitation. Me and weddings don't go well together," I say, as I smile and chuckle. "But good to see you, Jason. Call my office next week, and we can do lunch somewhere." Jason nods and pats me on the shoulder before waving to the crew of guys behind him to follow their server to their reserved table.

Spinning myself back around, I analyze my face in the bar's wall mirror. I'm looking a little worse for wear these days. I scrub my fingers over my heavy stubble, rake my fingers through the right side of my head to tame a wayward strand and decide I need a haircut and a proper shave. Maybe I'll grow a goatee instead of a beard, have the sides of my head trimmed tight and let the crown be a bit longer. I may not be twenty years old anymore, but they say forty is the new

17

thirty, and I'm ready for a bit of a change.

The bartender tips his chin toward me to question if I want a refill, and I place my palm in the air to indicate that I'm done. The receipt for my two drinks gets quickly slipped inside my jacket pocket. Sometimes I wonder if he's more familiar with my credit card than I am since I come here nearly every night for a top-up or a client meeting. I smile at him as I ease myself off the chair and head for the exit. I have an early showing of the property on Klassen Way, and I want to confirm with the showing agent, Daniella, that we're still on for the nine AM showing while I head to the subway.

My stride is quick. I think it might rain sooner than later, and if I have to jog the next four blocks to the station, I'll do it. The clouds appear to be moving swiftly across the evening sky tonight, and I wonder if a storm is brewing off the coast. Once I reach the station, I realize I've missed the 7:15 train and have to wait another ten minutes for the next one. I find an open seat on a bench and pull out my cell to check the weather reports for tomorrow morning and look through any emails I need to address.

I get distracted by a notification on Twitter from an artist I've been following recently. She's posted two new images of watercolour paintings. I enlarge each image to see them more clearly. I never cared much for watercolour paintings until I came across one of hers that another follower shared. There is something different about the way she paints that I find interesting. I've also noted that she does some sculpture work. Typically I'd be more interested in the sculptures, but her watercolours have caught my attention as well.

The train I need screeches to a halt in front of me, and I rise with the other waiting passengers to enter the car. Glancing around the open seats, I have to pick and choose which one I want that hopefully hasn't been pissed, puked, or spat on during the day. The third seat on my right looks the cleanest, and it's now mine.

Maybe it was the two double Bourbons I knocked back and

my empty stomach, but I have the undeniable urge to direct message her and ask her about where her work is displayed. Maybe she does this as a pastime, not as a profession. Maybe she is a professional and has her work on display in a gallery. Fuck. Why am I assuming she's in New York? She could be anywhere.

The car stops at the next station, and a load of people climb on and climb off in a jumbled mess of bumping shoulders, backpacks, and shuffling shoe sounds. I keep my head aimed down at my cell phone as I raise my eyes to take a glance around at the new passengers. There are only two more stops before I'm home, and I may have one more Bourbon when I get there.

The sun is about to set by the time I reach my apartment, but the heavy cloud cover and distant black clouds make it impossible to witness. I remember the first time I viewed this suite. It was about this same time of day, the skies were dappled with light cumulous clouds, the sun was setting, and while I marveled in the beauty of the views, I suddenly couldn't imagine myself living anywhere else. As I notice the impending storm brewing, I remember that storm watching from my suite is equally impressive.

After dropping my briefcase on the counter, my phone begins to buzz in my jacket. I pull it out to see the realty agent showing my listing tomorrow is confirming her appointment. Daniella is an excellent agent, and I never need her to confirm appointments, but it's my peace of mind that makes me do this regardless of the agent. She is one of the few you can count on one hundred percent of the time.

I find my bottle of Bourbon on the counter and collect a glass from the cabinet above me. A two-finger shot is all I need while I scan the Internet for a few hours. As I take the first sip of my drink, I recall the Twitter post about Olivia Aston's watercolour paintings. I'd like to know if her artwork is for sale somewhere online.

The Art of Love in New York City

I park my tired ass on the couch and flip open my laptop. Another quick sip of my Bourbon offers a slow burn down my throat, and I wince a little while I wait for the laptop to open up my apps. Twitter is always my first choice for information since many realtors use the app to market properties as I do.

There on the left side of the screen, I see the link to the notifications. The top notification is the one from Olivia's post. Now on a bigger screen, I can get a better look at her recent work. Stunning. I have no idea where she learned to do what she does, but it's so elegant. Forget it. You can't teach people to paint like that. This is pure unadulterated talent.

My fingers hover the mouse over her message link. "Yes, or no, Max?" I mutter aloud to myself. "Fuck it." I click the link and start randomly typing. I introduce myself, assure her I'm not a weirdo, and compliment her on her paintings. Wait. I back up and erase the weirdo comment. If I have to tell her I'm not a weirdo, she will naturally think I am one.

My last two sentences read: I'm interested to know if your paintings and sculptures are for sale and where an interested buyer like myself might view them in person. Do you have a gallery representing your work in New York?

I read my message three times before I hit the send arrow. Done. She probably won't respond anyway. I knock back the last of the Bourbon in my glass and flick on the television as I kick off my shoes and rest my feet atop the coffee table.

A good half hour passes before I see a few dots jumping on the message screen from Olivia. My feet slide off the coffee table, and I lean forward, awaiting her words to appear.

Olivia: "It seems we are both New Yorkers. There is a gallery in Manhattan that frequently show my sculptures and paintings. If you are truly interested, reply to me, and I'll send you the address to the gallery."

I flex my fingers and rub the edge of my chin. This is interesting. She is in New York. I respond immediately.

Me: "Hi. Thanks for replying. I'd love to visit the gallery. Please send me the name and address. I have some free time tomorrow afternoon, and I might be able to slip over for a viewing. Max.

Olivia: "That's wonderful."

She provides me the name and address for the gallery in the balance of her message. I'm not familiar with it, but I'm sure I'll find it. I questioned if I should continue a casual conversation with her, but I talk myself out of it. Another time. Tomorrow I'm going to sell a house and hopefully buy myself a sculpture for my entry hall.

Chapter 4 – Max

The drive out to Klassen Way for this morning's showing is a long one, but estates like these are more often on the outskirts of the city limits. Had this gem been located within New York's city boundaries, the price would be triple. But a nine-point five million asking isn't anything to sneeze at.

Once I've climbed out of my car, I catch a glimpse of the horses in the nearby pasture. I'd be curious to know if the interested buyers want lodging for horses or if the corrals, pastures, and paddocks will sit empty with new owners. The scene is charming. It's hard to believe that one can have this kind of country sanctuary for less than ten million within an hour's drive from the city.

Throwing on my jacket and grabbing my briefcase from the passenger seat, I head to the front door and retrieve the key from the lockbox. The family that owns this property has moved to Kentucky, where their other estate is located, so this house sits unoccupied and sparsely furnished.

One of the good things about a mostly empty house is that your voice echoes when you speak, giving the future buyer the impression that it is much larger than it first appears. I travel from room to room, flicking on the lights, checking for any wayward garbage, and ensuring each room is as presentable as possible. The house could use some updates, but it is move-in ready for the time being. The current owners were meticulous about maintaining this home, which saves me from hiring cleaning crews and landscapers to spruce the place for marketing purposes.

If I'm lucky, Daniella will have already pre-qualified these buyers right down to their favourite colours. Daniella is not only beautiful but a savvy realty agent with a sweet personality. If she were single, I'd be all over her trying to get inside those pink panties.

In reality, I have no idea what colour her panties are, but I imagine in my sex-craved mind they are pink. With lace. And her ass is tight as a drum. Jesus, what I wouldn't do to squeeze that ass of hers in my hands.

I shake my head and try to refocus on helping Daniella sell this property to her clients. I gave myself a semi thinking about her ass and other womanly assets, and this can't happen now. They will be here in ten minutes or so.

The last touch I need to add to the kitchen space is to open up the French-styled doors and draw up the wood blinds, so the view of the gardens and the pool is impossible to miss when the interested buyers enter the room. If this view doesn't sell her clients, nothing will.

I remind myself quickly of the list of outbuildings and other unique qualities of the property in my head, so I'm prepared to answer any questions without checking my notes.

Just as I exit the front doors, I see Daniella's car arriving up the long driveway. Perfect timing. I place my hands inside my pockets and wander slowly toward her car as she and her clients climb out. Daniella smiles at me, and my semi comes back to life. With my hands still in my pockets, I give my cock a nudge and internally tell it to back the fuck down, all while smiling back at her.

The clients step behind the car and cover their eyes to block out the bright sun highlighting the fields and horses. They spin slowly, soaking in the full body of the property, and chat quietly to each other. Daniella encourages them to come inside the house with that sweet voice and a hand wave.

I think these people are already sold on the house and just needed to see it with their own eyes. The tour lasts nearly an hour since there are so many outbuildings to show them. The current

23

owners left their golf carts to sell with the house, and it makes it much easier to show the balance of this property with them. I'm reasonably sure Daniella's clients are going to make an offer. If it is any amount over nine million, I can talk my sellers into taking it.

We arrive back in our golf carts to the main house, and Daniella's clients are all smiles. A damned fine sight that is. We shake hands, chat a bit, and then as the clients move toward Daniella's car, I have a quick conversation with her.

"I think you've found the right buyers," I say, and she smiles sweetly at me. I think I just blushed. Fuck me.

"Yes. I'm sure they're going to write an offer. I'll encourage them to put a dollar value on paper today, and I should have something to tell you later this afternoon. Are you back in town for the rest of the day?"

"Yes. I'm heading back to the office, and then I have a meeting at a gallery in Manhattan around one o'clock."

"Fine. We'll talk later today," she says, then waves at her clients as they climb inside her car. "I should head out then. Have a great afternoon."

I watch that amazing ass of hers wander off from me and chuckle. "You need to get yourself laid," I mumble to myself as I head back inside the house to close everything up and lock the front doors.

Chapter 5 – Olivia

"Hello, Livie," I hear Sasha's voice chime through my cell phone. "Are you coming in today to discuss next weekend's exhibit party?" she asks in her sing-song way.

"Good morning, Sasha. Yes, I'll be there at eleven. I have two smaller sculptures that I'd like to add to the exhibit, which I completed last week. Do you think you'll have space for them?" I ask.

"Of course! Your pieces are always welcome, Livie. How dare you even consider that you need to ask!" she says, attempting to scold me.

"I always ask, and I know you never say no. It's our thing, Sasha. Now, do I need to bring you anything before I arrive? Something to eat or drink?"

"No, Honey. Just bring your lovely self and your beautiful sculptures. I'll have wine chilling for you by the time you arrive. Come earlier if you can. I have a delivery of a rather large piece from Devlan Marx arriving, and I'd like you to help me decide where in the gallery it should be placed," she says.

"Okay. No problem. Ten-thirty it is. Bye."

As expected, the parking around Sasha's gallery is at a premium. I drive around the block three times before I catch someone leaving and can slip in behind them to take the highly coveted parking space. I'm right on time, which should please Sasha since she hates people who are late. Once parked, I grab the first of the two sculptures I have for exhibit and carry it inside. Sasha rushes to the front door to hold it open for me, and I peck her on her cheek as I pass her.

The Art of Love in New York City

"There is one more box," I say as I set the first sculpture down on the floor. "Hold the door. I'll be back in two seconds.

Once inside the gallery with my two new pieces, Sasha and I unbox them for her to inspect. "Livie, you never cease to amaze me. The glazing on this one is absolutely brilliant. I'm so excited to put these on display. Come. Let's figure out the layout for this weekend's exhibit party. The Devlan Marx piece hasn't arrived yet."

I nod and follow her to the reception desk, where her assistant is busy working on a spreadsheet on her laptop. "Good morning, Laila," I say as I approach the raised counter in front of it.

"Hi, Olivia," she chimes and gives me that bright smile of hers before going back to clicking her fingers over the keyboard entering sales data.

"Come, Livie. I have a list of the artwork in my office. That is also where the wine is chilling," she says, holding me by my shoulder and guiding me to her office.

Two hours later and three glasses of wine drunk, we have a layout planned for the exhibit. My pieces will be showcased near the front of the gallery window on the left side, along with two other artist's sculpture work. On the right side facing the other window, we'll place the Devlan Marx piece.

In the gallery's center, we'll arrange a large white marble table with hors d 'oeuvres, champagne, and a grand floral centerpiece. The back section of the gallery will be a mix of graphic art from an up and coming artist that Sasha met a few months ago. The small wing on the left of the studio will cater to craft art in fabrics from various local artisans. She acquired the shop space from next door when the business closed its doors and has expanded her gallery by an extra nine-hundred square feet.

"I think we've got it done, Sasha." She hands me another glass of wine, and I grimace at her. I'm not getting wasted before noon. You are such a bad influence," I tease as I take the glass from her hand and wink.

"Fine. Ask Laila to order lunch for us. And where the fuck did that delivery truck for the Marx piece go? You know how much I hate people being late."

I giggle and walk out of her office to chat with Laila. "Would you order some deli sandwiches for Sasha and me? She's getting growly without food in her belly," I joke.

"Yes. No problem," Laila replies.

I wander the exhibit space with my wine glass in hand. As I gaze up to the ceiling, I note the directional lighting might need to be changed to accommodate the sculptures' best spotlighting. I'll remind Sasha about the lighting since we forgot to do that for the last exhibit party.

Chapter 6 – Max

I send a quick text to my personal driver: "Harjit, I need you to meet me at the office in an hour. I'm going to need you to drive me to a gallery in Manhattan for one o'clock, and then I have two other potential listings to view at two-thirty and four-thirty."

"See you there, boss." My cell rings the second I end my call to my driver. The screen shows my assistant Clint's name, and I answer through my Bluetooth.

"Yes."

"Max, I have two offers on the 18th Street penthouse. The first is an all-cash deal with a ninety-day closing, but it's a bit of a lowball. The second offer is also lower than you want to hear, and it's got a subject on it. What time are you back in the office?"

"I'll be there in an hour. Text me the agent names on the offers and what the offers are, and I'll call them while I'm enroute."

I manage to get my calls in to the two agents making offers on the penthouse. The minimal from my seller is out by two-hundred thousand, and I doubt either of the interested parties are willing to go that high. I have to present these offers to my seller even if I already know they will be turned down.

Harjit gets me to the Lipinski Gallery at one o'clock sharp. I've not heard of this gallery before, and I take a minute to inspect the building's façade before I enter the gallery. The sparse number of exhibits surprises me, and I do a bit of a spin, wondering why there are only a few paintings on the walls. The receptionist greets me brightly with, "Welcome to the Lipinski Gallery. Have you been here before or is this your first visit?"

I smile and nod. "My first visit. I was told that an artist named

Olivia Aston exhibits here, and I've come to view her sculptures. But I see you're in the middle of some changes, or is the gallery always this sparse?"

"Oh, yes. We have an upcoming event this weekend. We're in the process of placing the new pieces for that exhibit. Olivia was here earlier. You've just missed her," she says as she reaches over the desk and retrieves the marketing materials for the upcoming exhibit. "I'm sorry you came in and were unable to see her work. She is very talented. Can you make it to the event this Saturday? It runs from one o'clock to nine."

I take the flyer from her hand and give it a glance. "Yes. I'll make a point of attending. Thank you." I turn on my heels and head outside to get back in my car. "Harjit?"

"Yes."

"Can I take you to lunch? Have you eaten yet?"

"No, I'm starved. Where do you want to go?" she asks.

"You choose. Anywhere is good for me. I've got some phone calls to make while you drive." It pisses me off a bit, knowing I just missed meeting Olivia Aston. I like to meet the artists of the pieces I buy. Their art means more to me when I know who the artist is personally. Perhaps on Saturday she will be there, and we can meet. Since her Twitter account doesn't show her face, only her latest work as her profile picture, I have no idea what to expect. My mind immediately conjures up a vision of her, drawn of nothing but her words to me and the kindness I sensed within them.

Chapter 7 – Olivia

I was still inside Sasha's office, enjoying my sandwich when the bell rang at the front door of the gallery. Sasha insisted that we stay inside her office and let Laila deal with the customer. Since the walls and display stands were mostly empty of art pieces, it was unlikely the customer would stay long.

"You should do all this rearranging during off-hours, Sasha. You may have missed an opportunity to make a sale, but you only have ten items on display."

"I don't have time in the evenings this week. Normally I would do all the setups after hours, but this week is a bitch for me. I've got guests from out of town until Friday afternoon. That doesn't give me enough time to set up the new exhibit in the evening before Saturday."

I agree and smile, then head out of her office to use the bathroom, where Laila notices me. Her eyes grow wide with surprise. "I thought you left already. There was a guy here asking about your work. Shit," she says as she plunks her bum into her office chair. "If I'd known you were still here, I'd have introduced you to him."

I look at her a bit shocked since nobody ever asks specifically to see my work. Then it dawns on me about the guy who inquired about me on Twitter. "Dammit! Did you invite him back for this weekend's event?" I'm a bit steamed now and place my hands on my hips.

"Yes. I gave him the flyer, and he said he'd come back. Maybe you can meet him then?"

I soften my stance and nod. I point at the security camera. "Is there footage of him coming in today that I can see?

"Yes. Come to my desk. I can access all the surveillance cameras from my laptop," she says, waving her hand to me to follow her.

Together Laila and I watch the last ten minutes of video capture footage and see him enter, chat with Laila, and leave. He's dark-haired, handsome from what I can tell on the screen, and wearing a rather expensive-looking suit, so now I can double-check on Twitter for his profile picture to confirm he's the man who directly messaged me.

"He was nicely dressed and polite."

I snicker at her and smile. I've seen guys who look like they are homeless come into the gallery, drop twenty-grand on an art piece like it were a two-dollar coffee without blinking an eye. What a person wears is not a true indicator of money or buyers of art. You should know this by now, Laila," I say and slap her gently on her shoulder.

Saturday arrives, and I'm having a bitch of a time deciding what to wear. It is still hot as hell outside, and this heatwave doesn't look like it's going to subside anytime soon. I decide on a simple white sheath dress, and a pair of white, open-toed four-inch high slingbacks. I'll bring a sweater in case the air conditioning gets too cold inside the gallery. I order a cab to drive me to the gallery and arrive just a few minutes before one o'clock.

Sasha's attention is occupied as the guests begin to filter inside. Most of the Lipinski Gallery patrons are regulars who know Sasha personally or are the artists themselves. She has an extensive list of art buyers, amassed over her twenty-two years at this location. Her husband's connections helped her get noticed more quickly than most new gallery owners, so she's been profitable since her first year in operation.

I was smart enough to eat a large meal before arriving, knowing Sasha will be refilling my champagne flute repeatedly throughout the afternoon. Being one of her favourite artists and one of my dearest friends means I won't be able to leave the event until she closes the doors at nine. She also knows I have nothing to go home to, and she'll use that excuse to ensure I stay until the last guest is gone.

I'll keep my eyes open all afternoon and late into the evening for the buyer named Max, who inquired about me earlier in the week. I have missed his arrival somehow, or he was unable to attend. Pity. I always enjoy meeting people who are interested in my work. I make a mental note to contact him on Twitter when I get home. With the champagne coursing through my veins, I'll be a little more forward and courageous in talking with a stranger than if I were sober.

And speaking of strangers, I see Sasha talking to a smartly dressed woman as they stand before one of my watercolour paintings. I make my way through the crowd and let myself be known. Sasha's eyes light up as I approach, and she gestures for me to meet one of the guests. "This is my dear friend Olivia, and the artist of this painting," she coos as the woman turns to meet me eye to eye.

"Call me Teddy."

Her confidence oozes as she shakes my hand and offers me a bright smile. Her long raven colored hair shines in the light of the room. Her lips are painted a deep red – a shade I could never pull off – and her pale green, almond-shaped eyes capture my attention when she fixes her gaze upon mine. There is something truly interesting about Teddy, and I find myself admiring everything about her in this first introduction.

"I love your work, Olivia," she says, and I smile and nod. Our eyes meet again, and in a strange way, I feel very drawn to her. Another smile slowly eases over her lips, and I feel like she sees me in a light that few others do. "I've decided to purchase this one," she says in her silky voice, and my heart skips a beat.

I place my hand over my heart and reply, "Oh, my God. Thank you."

"You are humble and talented," Teddy replies while gently grabbing my hand. "My favourite kind of people." The longer she talks and looks at me, the more I'm drawn to her. I've never felt an attraction to a woman before but Teddy is beautiful and has a confidence that is as admirable as it is sexy. I should probably stop drinking.

"How do you know Sasha?"

"Her husband Dimitri and my father, Lawrence Braithwaite do quite a bit of business together. My father and I are art collectors, so we rely on Sasha to curate the pieces we're most interested in. I have a weakness for watercolours. Your style is so elegant, and your subjects come to life in such a beautiful way. Now that I've met you, I can understand where that beauty comes from," she says as she clinks her glass to the rim of mine.

I'm not used to being told I'm special in any way, and so I soak up her compliments and unintended physical attraction like a sponge. Before I have a chance to decline, Sasha is refilling my champagne flute and suggesting that she mingle with the other guests while I get more acquainted with Teddy.

Within the next two hours, I find myself having difficulties standing in my heels, and Teddy and I decide to hide in Sasha's office for a little while. We kick off our shoes and sit across from each other in the two guest chairs in front of Sasha's office desk with a bottle of

The Art of Love in New York City
champagne and our flutes in hand.

What Teddy has over me isn't immediately clear, but I cannot leave her side willingly. Her mannerisms are quite sensual, and my surprising attraction to her is not fading.

"Tell me about yourself, Teddy. Are you married?"

"Not anymore. I love shoes, art, and restaurants far too much to be barefoot in the kitchen, waiting for my significant other to arrive home from work."

That comment makes me giggle. "So, no men in your life currently?"

"The one's I've dated recently seem more like boys than men. I prefer my men to be like a good wine. One that ages nicely, and it knows how to finish well." Teddy's brilliant smile flashes before she sips from her flute. "But my interests in companions varies. And how about you?"

I adjust my position and a hint of hesitation in my voice can be heard when I answer, "I married my college professor nineteen years ago, but I may as well not be married now."

"Oh. Well, that sounds tragic." Teddy's eyes narrow, showing me her honest concern. "So no contact at all?"

I smile trying to lighten the mood but my next words don't match my expression. "It's been a long time since he's touched me."

Teddy leans forward and her eyes lock on mine. In a near whisper she asks, "Olivia. When was the last time the professor gave you an oral exam?"

I hesitate to answer that question with honesty, but somehow I trust her to be discrete. "Never. Not once," I admit (in a hushed voice) while gently shaking my head side to side.

"Never?"

"Nope."

"Oh, Livie." Teddy's free hand gently waves above her head as she offers her shocked expression. "You're an artist! How can you paint the heavens if you've never seen stars before?" She takes my right hand and interlaces her fingers into mine. She lets out a long, soft breath and raises her flute in front of me. "Here's to new experiences, Livie."

We clink glasses, and then Teddy wraps the arm holding her glass around the hand holding mine. As we drink from our respective glasses, the positioning of our arms forces us to pull our faces closer together.

"I bet your champagne tastes better," Teddy says. Then she inches forward and gives me a gentle kiss. I could feel my entire body awakening as her mouth glanced my lips.

As I pull away, I squeeze her hand back and feel my face flush a bit at her gesture. Is it the champagne that is making me feel a strange sexual attraction to Teddy, or is there something more to this?

As we continue to talk, Teddy makes me laugh heartily at her curious observations about the world. We talk at length about art, and she tells me about some of the pieces in her home. It sounds as if she lives in a modern museum.

I find her love of art and her sense of humor intoxicating. It makes me feel as if I've known Teddy for years. Refreshing as it may be to connect with another woman this way, the lustful emotions I feel for her are very real. Sasha and I have that kind of connection, but with Teddy, there is a sexual note that I can't deny is making me question myself. I offer Teddy a bright smile and stand to clear my head and rearrange my thoughts.

Sasha enters her office to reprimand us for escaping the event for so long and to remind us that it is over, and she'd like to go home.

"Oh, so early?" I grumble and give Sasha a playful pouty face.

"Come now, Livie. You've had too much champagne, and you should go home too." Sasha takes my arm and begins to usher me to the door of the office.

"Olivia, I can give you a ride," Teddy asks as she rises from her chair and attempts to insert her toes back into her shoes.

"That isn't necessary, Teddy," Sasha says sternly. The volume of her voice sobers me for a moment. "I've got a cab waiting outside for Livie."

Teddy turns to me and winks. "Livie. Are you sure you want to go home, or would you like to see some of the art I told you about?"

My eyes widen by the prospect. I'm not ready to go home yet. Maybe it isn't such a good idea to carry on, but I'm feeling too good to let my evening end here. I'm happy, and I deserve to be happy. I don't think I've let myself be so free and silly and connected with another person in what feels like forever. Teddy is like a drug, and I want more of whatever it is she's offering.

"It's settled then. Olivia is coming for a tour of my collection. Gather your things while I text Nathanial to bring the car around," Teddy states as she squeezes past Sasha's shoulder to enter the main hallway.

Sasha holds me by the elbow as I pick up my shoes from the floor and sling my purse precariously over my left shoulder. "Livie, you should go home. You and Teddy can get together again some other time. Have lunch or something another day," Sasha suggests.

Her brows are pinched at me while she tries to convince me I'm too drunk to make wise choices.

"Stop, Sasha," I say as I press her shoulder gently with my hand. "I'm fine. Thank you for letting us crash your office," I add, trying not to slur my words to prove I'm perfectly good to continue my evening with Teddy.

"Fine. Do what you like, but call me tomorrow," she says, sounding a bit hurt. I don't get why she has shifted into motherly mode all of a sudden.

The two of us have a good laugh at our state of drunkenness as we exit the gallery and a tall thin man in a dark suit guides me into the back of Teddy's limo. I look back to see Sasha locking up the gallery and walking over to her awaiting car and driver. She gives me a quick look, and I wave and blow her an air kiss. Sasha reaches into the air to pretend to catch it before slipping inside her car.

"I had a feeling you wanted to leave with me for an adventure," I hear Teddy say, and I nod and giggle in blissful drunken agreement. As the limo drives away, Teddy slides up close to me and clasps my hand in hers. Sasha's words from five minutes ago repeat in my head, and I wonder briefly if I should heed her advice and have Teddy take me back to my apartment.

While I convince myself that Sasha is right, Teddy's hand slips from mine and gently rubs across my thigh in a slow up and down motion. Then her hand slips under the linen fabric of my dress and rises between my thighs just an inch from my sex. Anticipating that she was going further, I sit straighter in the seat, giving myself another inch of space, bringing Teddy's hand to a stop where it is. Her touch is heavenly regardless of what I can't immediately make of where her hand has landed.

I lay my head back upon the headrest of the plush white

leather seat of the limo and close my eyes for a moment. I try to recall the last time Carl's hand slipped between my thighs, and I cannot. It has been too long since I've felt a hand, any hand caress my skin in such a beautiful way. Am I so desperate to be touched now that I don't care whose hand is on my thigh?

Teddy's fingers edge closer, and within seconds my body is reacting, and I'm damp from her touch. She leans forward to slide her bum a little off the seat and holds a heady stare into my eyes. "Do you mind if I touch you here?" she whispers. I shake my head to indicate no. A smile eases over Teddy's full lips, and then a barely-there kiss is placed upon mine.

I feel like I'm Alice in Wonderland, falling down the rabbit hole in slow motion. Where I land is anybody's guess as I have lost all my ability to push Teddy back from her advances. Nothing more than the tender touch and the kiss happens. Teddy leans back into her seat and squeezes my hand in hers again.

We arrive at Teddy's palatal apartment in what seems like only a few minutes, but I think the time is passing me by more quickly now that my attention has been taken elsewhere. With her clasped hand in mine, she leads me to her living room. I find her perfume invigorating, her affections so desperately needed, and once again, I'm wrestling with myself over my swift physical connection to her. "Would you like something to drink, Olivia?" she asks as she clasps both of my hands in hers, knowing I'm still a bit unstable on my feet as she lets me sit down on the couch.

I nod. "Yes. Water, please. My head is spinning and I don't think more alcohol is a wise choice."

"We all know our limits. Water it is." Teddy saunters her way to the bar on the left side of the living room to fill a glass with water for me. While she's busy, my eyes soak in the clean lines and the pure white surroundings. My eyes land on an oil painting by Marianne Trombley next to an Acacia Palm set in a large white concrete planter, and I have to squint a bit to focus my eyes. "Is that what I think it is?"

"Yes. You are familiar with Marianne Trombley? I acquired it several years ago. Delightful, isn't it?" Teddy asks as she returns to me with a glass of cold water.

I take a sip of the water and smile at her. *Delightful indeed and outrageously expensive,* I think to myself. "Your taste in art is quite eclectic. Is that on purpose or do you have specific objects in mind to acquire?"

"Not intentional in the least. I buy most items because I like them, but a few have been purchased for the investment value such as the Trombley abstract. That one is titled…"

I interrupt Teddy and speak her words for her. "45-23."

"Yes," Teddy says and nods. You *are* familiar with her work."

"She has an unusual system for titling her pieces. Her age and the day she completes it. Therefore this piece was created while she was forty-five and it was the twenty-third day of the month.

Teddy nods again and her pretty smile lands upon me. "My father is the investment collector, I do it for pleasure. And you, my darling Olivia, give me great pleasure," she says as her body leans closer to mine and my senses become flooded by her sensual perfume.

I redirect my focus on the surroundings once again. It is surprisingly calming for such a stark space but perhaps it is the plush fabrics that stave off the harshness that an all-white decor can bring. Once again, my thoughts are interrupted by Teddy's hand on my knee as she sits beside me and hands me the water glass.

"What do you think?" she asks.

The Art of Love in New York City

I take another healthy drink of the water before replying, "About what?"

"My decorating choices. Your eyes were wandering around the room, but your face stayed expressionless. Does that mean you approve or disapprove?" Her smile is soft as she sips another glass of spirits.

"It's sublime, like you," I say as I flick my gaze to her face.

"Is that so," she replies, and a beautiful smile eases over her full red lips. Teddy sets her glass upon the coffee table and clasps my hand in hers. "Olivia," she says, tilting her head a little as she forms her next thought. "You are not only a truly talented artist, but you are also a beautiful soul. I can't say that about many women, certainly not the ones I spend most of my time with."

My eyes search hers. Am I reading the room right? I swear the air in the space between us just became heavier or is it that I'm breathing heavier. My eyes search hers again, and her smile has not faded. I'm drawn to her confidence, her voice and her touch. But is that all I'm drawn to?

Teddy leans in, and her lips grace mine again as they did in the limo. I am not disappointed. Is this what I truly want? To explore my sexuality with a stranger, a woman, and while drunk on champagne? All I want is to be loved and now I'm willing to take that love from anyone.

I eagerly follow her to the bedroom. Our bodies spoon together within the silk sheets of her bed. She holds me tight, kissing the nape of my neck while my breaths slowly calm to a normal pace after she treated my body to multiple, wonderful, orgasms. Somehow she seemed to understand that I needed this encounter more than I realized it myself.

I've sobered up a bit since we left the gallery. My state of bliss has reached new levels in her hands, and I'm compelled to explore her body the way she explored mine. All my previous boundaries have fallen to the wayside as I take the lead. I turn my body within the silk sheets to face her and begin to kiss Teddy passionately. My hands caress her breasts as her nipples peak high, and I draw my mouth toward them, gently licking and sucking on them in the same way she did mine.

"You should know that I've never done this before," I murmur, "But I want to return the favor."

"I know, Olivia," she says softly while her perfectly manicured nails stroke gently through my hair. It is part of the reason you excite me, but there is so much more to you than I bargained for. You're a work of art in every way."

The softness of her skin, combined with the sultriness of her voice, continue to intoxicate me as I move my mouth down her torso, inhaling the scent of what lingers of her perfumed body lotion. She lays down, arches her back and closes her eyes. As my body hovers over hers, I reach my hand between the silky soft skin of her inner thighs and let my fingers spread her wetness for me over her aching sex. She and I gaze into each other's eyes, and we smile in unison, understanding that what we are sharing is wonderful. I don't know that I'd let another woman seduce me the way Teddy has. This is not who I am – this is just who I am tonight.

I slip two slick fingers inside of her and watch her face as my moves bring her pleasure. I'm liking having this control over her body, seeing her eyes flutter as I repeatedly press inside of her. Teddy grips one hand over my arm as the sounds of her moans grow louder the closer she comes to her release. In the last few moments of her building orgasm, I place my mouth over her entrance and sucked gently upon her clit while I continued to use my fingers to tip her over the edge. Her moans change to whimpers just before she comes for me.

41

The Art of Love in New York City

There is a strange satisfaction that overcomes me knowing I brought her to a place of bliss. I gave her what she gave me, and she loved it. Teddy pulls me up close to her and the most beautiful smile beams back at me. She devours my mouth, and my heart pounds in unexpected ways. "You are a natural," she murmurs as I place my fingers over my lips and taste them then Teddy cracks up at me.

"I think you may have enjoyed that more than you anticipated," she says, and I cannot help the bashful smile that forms along with a flush to my cheeks. It was beautiful, meaningful, special. I lay back down beside her and listen to her soft breaths. They calm me while my eyes close as the need to sleep overpowers me.

When I awake in the morning, I am groggy, and my head is pounding. I expected to have some repercussions from my excessive alcohol consumption, but this headache is nasty. Beside me, sleeping like an angel in this pure white bedroom, is the woman who I spent the night with. If I'm supposed to be ashamed of myself, that emotion escapes me. I feel amazing and have no regrets. I consider waking Teddy up, but it might be best to let her rest.

I slip as silently as I can from the silk sheets, scanning the room for my clothes as I rise to my feet and find them scattered across the floor at the foot of the bed. I manage to get myself dressed and cleaned up enough to go out in public without looking like a complete mess. There is a notepad on the side table, and I take the opportunity to leave Teddy a message. *"You were beautiful to me last night. Thank you. O.A."*

My purse is also on the nightstand beside sleeping beauty. I gently lift it off the side table and scan the room one last time to make sure I've not forgotten anything before I make my silent escape for home. Thankfully, my cell phone has enough charge left to call for an Uber, and I make that request as I slip out of this amazing apartment and reach the elevator.

As I climb inside my Uber driver's car, I begin to recall a few more fragments of what transpired last night. I was treated well by Teddy, and I gave myself freely to her, unabashedly so, because she made it so easy for me to let myself be loved by another.

Chapter 8 – Max

It pissed me off to no end that I wasn't able to attend the Lipinski Gallery event on Saturday. I spent nearly the entire day negotiating with my seller and the two parties that had offers on the penthouse, not to mention another deal fell through that I was sure was completed. Some days you can't win, I remind myself.

I arrive back to my apartment by nine o'clock. I'd thought about going to the bar, but that place is a zoo on Saturday nights, and I wasn't in the mood to deal with drunks and loud music.

Checking in on Twitter, I noticed most of the accounts I converse with were offline. No surprise there. I liked a few tweets and was just about to put the phone down on the counter when I saw a direct message light up. It appears I had disappointed Olivia by not showing up for the gallery showing today. "How did she know I wasn't there?" I question aloud. I think for a minute and try to figure that question out before I reply.

Me: I had a hectic day. How did you know I wasn't there?

Olivia: We had a guest book, and I didn't see your name appear on it.

Me: Was it well attended?

Olivia: Yes. Sasha Lipinski has many friends in the art world. Never a dull moment at her gallery exhibit events.

Me: When is the next one? I promise to attend.

Olivia: She does one a month except for August. She takes holidays then. The next one will be the first week of September.

Me: I'll add it to my calendar now. In the meantime, is there anywhere else that your sculptures are on exhibit or for sale?

Olivia: No. Unless you come to my studio in my home, you won't see them anywhere else.

Me: Why only one gallery?

Olivia: Sasha is my best friend. She's the only one I trust to display and market my work. I do this for pleasure rather than for income.

Me: Tragedy. Your work is beautiful. Do you have a website?

Olivia: No, Sasha has my work on her website. You can go to Lipinskigallery.com for a viewing of her current collection. There is also a page for people requesting commissioned pieces by specific artists if that interests you.

Me: Thanks. Only your work interests me at this time.

Olivia: That's very kind. What sort of pieces are you looking for? Sculptures or watercolours?

Me: At the moment, sculptures. However, I have become a fan of your watercolours. They would make great housewarming gifts for my clients.

Olivia: What is your profession?

Me: I own and operate a real estate company. Max Donovan Realty. I have a satellite office in Los Angeles as well, which is run by my brother Russell.

Olivia: Impressive. When you mentioned buying artwork as gifts for your clients, do you have a budget?

Me: It depends on the client.

The Art of Love in New York City

Olivia: I see. My paintings sell for no less than ten thousand through Sasha. My sculpture pricing depends on how long it took me to complete them and how large they are.

Me: Sounds reasonable. At the moment, I'm looking for a sculpture to place in the entry hall of my apartment. Not too large. A statement piece, if you will. Is there any way we could have this conversation over the phone? I'm not a fan of texting. She doesn't reply immediately. She may have been taken aback by my request. After a few minutes, she replies. Her phone number pops up on my screen, and I smile. That was far easier than I expected.

Me: Can I call you now, or would you rather I spoke with you on Monday during regular business hours?

Olivia: I'm free now if you are.

"Well, you don't have to ask me twice!" I say aloud to my empty apartment. I reach across my coffee table and pick up my phone. Glancing back at my laptop screen for her number, I begin dialing. The phone rings three times before I hear her answer, "This is Olivia Aston."

I smile again. "Hello, Olivia. This is Max. Are you sure it's okay for me to be calling you at this time of night?

"Yes. It's fine. I'm just sitting in my studio, looking out the window to the street below. You are a welcome distraction."

"Good to know."

I find the Lipinski gallery website on my laptop and the link to Olivia's work. I stumble a bit for something to ask her. She sounds melancholy, like she's tired, and I feel like I've imposed on her when I shouldn't have.

"So, you wanted to discuss sculptures? Is that correct?" Her voice lingers in my ears. It's melodic, confident, and sexy as hell.

Maybe calling her was a bad idea.

"Yes. I like the Bonsai tree piece you tweeted a picture of last week. How big is it, and is it sold yet?"

"Oh. No, it hasn't found a home yet. I think that one is about twenty-six inches tall and nearly as wide. I titled that piece Patience. Sasha will have the exact specifications. I don't measure my work as I create it. To me, scale is visual, not a number. Does that make sense or did that make me sound a bit vapid?" she giggles. My ears perk up again at her laughter. Jesus, I wish I knew what she looked like and how old she was. It would be rude to ask her age. I'll have to guess it when I finally meet her. I laugh with her and assure her she is anything but vapid.

"Have you been a New Yorker all your life?" I ask, taking our conversation to a more personal level. My body relaxes a little now that I know she is not uncomfortable talking with me.

"Yes. I was raised upstate but moved to the city for college and never left. I married shortly after graduation to one of my instructors. He's ten years older than I, and we weren't messing around during my schooling – to be clear. We met again after I graduated, and we married only seven months after our first date."

"I came close to marrying once," I admit, (breathe out a heavy breath). For whatever reason, I'm disappointed that she's married. Fine. I'll admit the reason. She's garnered my attention on several levels now. She's a brilliant talent, she's educated, and her voice's timbre completely arouses me. I remind myself to keep the personal conversation to a minimum and attempt to go back to asking her questions about her art. "What made you decide on watercolours and sculpture over other mediums?"

"That is a mighty fine question, Max."

The Art of Love in New York City

I can hear a smile in her voice when she replies to my question.

"I think I liked sculpting because I loved the feel of the clay in my hands. I felt very much in control. That feeling has never left me, and to this day, it is my favourite medium. The watercolours are secondary for me, but I like having an escape from sculpting on occasion. Just something to mix it up a bit, clear my mind, if you will." She pauses before she asks me, "Why real estate?"

"Family business. My father was an agent for twenty-seven years. My brother and I followed in his footsteps. I started my own agency about six years ago with my brother. When his wife transferred to LA for work, we opened up another agency there. I am the owner of both offices, and Russell is my managing director for the LA branch."

"That must keep you exceptionally busy. Do you travel to the LA office frequently?"

I hear the sounds of her sorting through her art supplies. It is as if she is putting things away in cupboards and rinsing out containers. I lean back into the depth of my couch and consider pouring myself a glass of wine. Speaking to Olivia is relaxing. Our conversation is not as strained as it should be since this is our first one on one.

The thing that strikes me is that if she's spent any time looking at my tweets, she'll know what I look like, but none of her tweets contain images of her.

"I do travel there several times a year, but I try to let Russell have full control. If I go there, it is more for a vacation from the hustle and bustle that is New York, and not specifically for business."

The sounds of her rustlings have subsided now. A glance at my watch tells me we've been texting and talking for nearly half an hour, and I think it might be time to let her off the hook. "Should I let you go?" I ask. I want her to say no, but I'll accept whatever her decision is.

"Oh. I didn't realize the time. If you have to go, then I guess this is goodnight."

I hear the hesitation in her voice, and it makes me smile. She doesn't want to hang up any more than I do. "I don't have any specific plans for this evening. I've enjoyed our conversation so far. I was worried you needed to attend to other things and that you may be too polite to tell me to call it a night."

I hear her beautiful laughter again. Silence follows, and then she speaks. "It's not often I have this long of a conversation with a perfect stranger about my artwork. It is refreshing to know that you have so much interest. And, at this moment, I needed a friend to chat with. I don't mind talking with you a bit longer if you don't."

"Will your husband be upset that you are talking to a man at this late hour?" I had to ask.

"I am still married, but Carl and I are separating in the coming weeks. This is all very new for us." She pauses while I try to think of something to say that doesn't sound overly sympathetic or, fuck, I don't know – weird? She speaks again before I do. "Carl had a stroke ten months ago. The resulting issue is that his personality has changed dramatically. Who knew that something like this would be a repercussion of a stroke? Anyway, he asked me for a divorce earlier this week, and so it is just a matter of deciding what happens next, I suppose," she says softly, then lets out a long sigh.

Now I feel like a complete asshole. This is such personal information, and I have no idea how to respond to her. I clench my jaw and pinch the space between my brows with my fingers while I think of something to say in response. "I'm very sorry to hear that," is all I can muster.

(She laughs softly). "I shouldn't have dumped that on you. What was I thinking? How rude of me to throw you into my personal life's trash bin. I'm sorry, Max. You seem to be a very nice guy, and talking to you somehow feels easy. Maybe I'm too tired to think clearly about personal boundaries. My apologies."

I sit up straight and knit my brows. "No, no. It's fine. You needed to tell somebody, and I happen to be the one you said it to. We've all been through breakups, and so I completely understand where your head is. Don't worry about it," I offer as calmly as I can. I am quite sincere, and now I am worried about her. God, this is ridiculous. I want to rush over to her and hold her while she cries it out. How fucking weird is that?

Without either of us realizing it, hours pass while we chat openly about relationships, people we've connected with on Twitter, and things we find amusing about everyday life. At midnight I begin to yawn. Not because the conversation is drying up but because I'm exhausted. She must have heard me yawn, and I hear her yawn back.

I break out into a hearty laugh, and she responds with a few giggles. "It's late, Max. We should both get some rest. I'll touch base with you in a few days about the Patience sculpture after I've let Sasha know you are interested. Is that alright?"

"Yes, yes, of course. Thank you for the conversation, Olivia. You made my evening far more interesting than I expected it would be. Sleep well."

"Yes, sleep well, Max. Goodnight."

Chapter 9 – Olivia

The distance between Carl and me has grown wider since he asked for a divorce. I try to stay out of his way as much as he tries to stay out of mine. It's the most ridiculous thing I've ever lived through, but until the divorce documents are agreed upon and issued to me by his legal counsel, this is the game we play.

I spoke to Sasha about the Patience sculpture this morning, and we agreed to lower the selling price to twelve thousand from fourteen thousand. I have no idea how much money Max is willing to spend on his statement piece for his entry hall, but if he balks, that's fine. I send him a message via Twitter to indicate what Sasha and I agreed upon, and now I wait for his reply.

Several hours pass before I see Max has read my message. He doesn't respond immediately, and so I assume the price was out of his range. That's okay. I still enjoyed talking with him and appreciated his compliments on my creations. An hour later, I get a phone call from Sasha. "Livie! You sold a piece today!" she sings to me in her light-hearted way.

"Really? Which one?"

"Patience. It sold to a very handsome man who was familiar with your work. He said he's been trying to buy a sculpture of yours for a while but was only now available to complete a purchase. Congratulations, Livie!"

My face lights up like a Christmas tree, and then I feel the heat of a blush flash over my skin. I know who purchased Patience. "Was the buyer's name Max Donovan?"

"Yes! How did you know?"

"He's a connection on Twitter and commented about that piece a while back. I guess he decided to buy it after all," I say, trying to downplay the fact that I'm dying to hang up on Sasha and direct message Max on Twitter to thank him.

"Well, whatever! We have a sale. And there was interest in your church watercolour as well, but I haven't heard back from the interested party. Fingers crossed we get another one of your pieces sold soon."

"Okay, okay. Don't get that excited. You know I don't do this for the money, Sasha. But it is nice to sell my artwork here and there. Mind you, I don't know how I'll fare financially when Carl and I officially part ways. At this point every sale counts more than it ever did." I pause and take in a deep breath at my realization that money is an issue I've rarely had to be concerned about. "Listen, I have to run some errands. Can we talk later?"

"Yes. Have a wonderful day, Livie. I'm so happy for you."

I swear she gets more excited over selling my art than I do. I scroll through my incoming calls on my phone and find Max's number. My finger hovers over the call icon, and then as if my finger had a mind of its own, I hit the icon, and my phone is suddenly dialing Max. I lick my lips and nervously fuss with my hair while I wait for him to answer. I should have messaged him on Twitter instead.

Unfortunately, I get his voicemail. That was very much a letdown. I was excited to thank him this morning. My words stumble from my lips as I say, "Hi. I just thought I'd phone to thank you for the purchase. Call me when you have a free minute. Bye."

After I hung up, I stared down at my phone screen and laughed at myself. I sounded like an idiot. Oh well, what's done is done. With my nervous energy coursing through me, I feel the need to have a bite to eat. Since Carl is still in bed, and I no longer have to quote, 'treat him like a small child', he can fend for himself for all his meals. While I make a small bowl of cereal and sit at the kitchen island bar, I decide on the things I absolutely want in the divorce. Number one is this apartment. I'll have to get an appraisal of its value and give him half of it to buy him out. He cannot have any furniture except his bedroom and that god-awful chair he likes to sit in to play his guitar in the living room. We already have separate bank accounts, so splitting money isn't necessary. But what should I ask for in alimony? I guess that is my plan today. I'll talk to my dad and have one of his lawyers draw up a divorce settlement agreement.

Chapter 10 – Max

It is just after seven in the morning when my phone starts ringing. I'm still in the shower and trying to wake up, so whoever is calling will have to leave a message. I get the feeling today is going to be one where I'm run off my feet.

I'm expecting the sale on Klassen Way to be completed this afternoon. The offer came in at just over nine million, which pleased the fuck out of my sellers. I must remember to send Daniella a gift basket for her work on finding the perfect buyer so quickly.

My phone rings again as I towel dry my hair and inspect my face for any spots that I missed with my razor. I hit the answer and speaker buttons on my cell and say, "Yes."

"Max. I have a new client with an apartment that he wants to sell. This client wanted to know if you could meet with him today at eleven," Clint says.

I lean forward toward the mirror and inspect my teeth quickly before I reply. "If there is nothing else on today's schedule for that time slot, then book it. Text me the address, please. Is there anything else, or can I get dressed now and head into the office without any further interruptions?"

"No. You're good. See you when you get in."

Between the forty-some odd emails and text messages I sort through this morning at the office, I find my coffee goes cold before I've had more than two sips of it. Most days, I'm pulled in multiple directions, and I like the juggling act I perform each day, but today I'm really not into it. I may need to take another trip to LA for a breather. A four-day weekend should do the trick.

Harjit sends me a quick text to let me know she's outside the building, waiting to take me to the eleven o'clock appointment with a potential new client. I grab my jacket, question if I should take a sip of my cold coffee, change my mind, and place my cell phone in my jacket pocket. I reach my car out front where Harjit stands to hold the door for me. She doesn't need to do this as I'm perfectly capable of opening the car door, but she seems to think it's part of her job. I give her an air kiss as I climb inside, and she laughs at me.

We reach the appointment with five minutes to spare. Parking is a bitch, so Harjit drops me off out front and then moves along to find a parking space to wait for me. I ring the buzzer to unit 418 and wait for a reply. No voice registers through the speaker. Only the long buzz of the door unlocking to let me enter the building is heard.

I recall how well maintained the building is. I've sold a few units over the years here, and it has a good reputation for being clean and centrally located to shopping, parks, and all levels of transit.

I knock three times on the door of suite 418 and wait. My phone rings in my pocket, and I pull it out, turn off the ringer, and ignore the call. As the sound of the lock unlatching catches my attention, an older man opens the door and nods at me. "Hi. I'm Max Donovan. I understand you are interested in selling your apartment, and I'm here to discuss it with you. You contacted my office to book the appointment." I say, reaching my hand out to shake his.

The man doesn't shake my hand, and I swiftly retract mine. He nods and gestures for me to enter the suite. I remove my shoes and take a glance around. As with many older buildings, the rooms are large and have some unique details. He leads me into his kitchen, and when he finally speaks, he asks me if I want coffee or tea.

"Tea, please. Unless you already have coffee made."

"I'll make some tea. I'm interested to know what my

apartment is worth as I may be selling it. But only if the price is right. Otherwise, I'll stay here," he says as he puts the electric kettle on to boil and pulls out two coffee cups from the cupboard above him.

"I've sold a couple of units in this building in recent years. They sell quickly because of the location. What number did you have in mind, or have you not put that much thought into it yet?" I ask.

"That is your job, isn't it?" he replies with a deadpan expression.

"Yes, of course." I open my briefcase and pull out the comparable sales in the area and the most recent sale information in this building. "I have sales data for this building and others nearby. Do you mind showing me around so I can gauge the views and the condition of your home for evaluation?" He nods again and gestures for me to follow him. We view each room briefly. I take note of the view aspect from each room and the overall condition of the unit.

It hasn't been updated for at least fifteen years, and that might put a damper on the value compared to the last unit sold in this building, which was completely renovated before it went on the market. The den is covered from ceiling to floor on all four walls with books on shelves. It makes me think he's either a professor or a writer. I want to ask him more questions, but he seems reluctant to talk openly or casually.

Next, he leads me upstairs to a second floor. "This is unusual," I say.

"My wife needed space for her work, and we purchased the suite above for her art studio and guest suite quarters. What I'm selling is actually two apartments."

When we reach the second floor, he shows me the adjustments they made. The kitchen has been removed, and so has the wall between the master bedroom and the kitchen to open up a huge area as an artist studio. "Great space and the light is amazing," I say.

I continue to wander the studio, until I stop dead in my tracks when I see a partially completed watercolour painting on an easel, several other paintings leaning against the walls, and a clay-coated workstation with a work in progress sculpture to the right of the painting. The obvious question is burning in my head. "Is your wife's name Olivia by any chance?"

He nods and looks me square in the eyes. "Yes. Are you familiar with her artwork?"

I try to hide my smile when I realize I'm in Olivia's studio. Why isn't she here? Dammit! We've missed crossing paths again. "Yes. I have seen your wife's artwork before. In fact, I own one of her sculptures. She is exceptionally talented." I walk over to the stack of paintings lining the floor under the large windows of the studio space. "May I?" I ask as I stand before them.

"Sure. Knock yourself out," he says. I gently flip through the paintings, one by one, hoping that she may have created a self-portrait, but I don't find what I'm looking for. I leave the conversation about her art closed and suggest that he and I settle in the living room to discuss pricing the two units for sale as one package or possibly dividing the two apartments again to sell them off separately. The situation I've found myself in now makes the conversation that Olivia and I had make sense. This is a divorce sale. These types of listings are often difficult as divorcing couples don't agree on many things, including what is an acceptable offer on jointly owned property. I force a smile over my lips and pretend I'm oblivious to their private life.

After Carl serves me my tea and sits in a ratty old rocking chair that looks entirely out of place from the rest of the furnishings, we discuss pricing. He's not much for elaborative conversation, and it makes it difficult to feel comfortable dealing with him. Within ten minutes, he's agreed to market both suites, as is, no separation for three and a half million. "Not a penny less," (he adds rather sternly).

I nod and attempt to shake his hand again. This time he obliges my gesture. I'll have my assistant draw up the listing paperwork this afternoon and deliver it to you. Once you've signed on as a client, I'll begin marketing your apartment immediately. Carl nods yet again as he sets his teacup on the top of his thigh and gazes out the window behind me.

"Do you think you can show yourself out?"

"Yes, of course. Thank you for the tea and the opportunity to sell your apartments. I promise you won't be disappointed with our services." I take my teacup with me and set it on the kitchen island as I pass through to the front door and let myself out of the suite. Carl is a peculiar man. I wonder if this is what Olivia was referencing when she said his personality had changed since the stroke.

Chapter 11 – Olivia

With another hot summer day predicted in the weather forecast, I decide to get an early start to my errands. I'd rather be inside my air-conditioned studio later today when the humidity adds insult to injury. "I should be back in my studio just past noon if all goes according to plan," I think to myself as I stuff my cell phone inside my purse and head out the door.

The beauty of having the entire second floor to myself is that I also have an entry from the fifth floor of the building. And to get a bit of exercise when I can't go for a run, I take the stairs as often as possible.

Surprisingly, my errands don't take me as long as I thought they would, which gave me enough time to enjoy a fresh garden salad and a glass of wine at the bistro next to the grocery store. I don't often treat myself to lunch in a place where I sit at a table, and people watch out of the window beside me. This is nice, really nice. I should do this more often. After I've finished my salad, I check a few emails, read some tweets on Twitter, and post a tweet about selling my Patience sculpture to a prominent New York real estate agent. I smile as I hit the send button, and I hope that Max sees the tweet and responds with a like and possibly a share.

It's now closing in on one o'clock, and the heat has risen to the ranks that were predicted. I cheerfully pay for my meal and tip my server, then head back to my car for the drive to my apartment. I remind myself not to let grumpy-pants Carl get on my nerves when I return. It would be nice if he'd escape the apartment every once in a while, but now that his classes are out of session at the University, he does virtually nothing with his spare time to read.

While I restock the cupboards and fridge with the groceries I'd purchased, Carl stays out of my way, opting to read a book in his den. I cannot believe how angry I am with him today. It seems like all my pent-up feelings over what has transpired recently has come to a head. I'm not only angry, but I'm bitter as well. This isn't how my life was supposed to be. We were supposed to grow old together, retire, and travel to far-flung places and enjoy the last half of our lives without a care in the world.

With the last of my restocking done, I take out a wine glass from the cabinet and fill it with a Sauvignon Blanc Sasha got me hooked on. I'm going upstairs to drink my wine, play some music, and work on my new sculpture. My art is my only constant now as everything else in my life has become fragmented.

I didn't hear the doorbell ring downstairs. In my own little world, I was now on my third glass of wine today, blissfully building my latest clay creation. I feel like I'm on a roll with this new piece, as I can completely envision it in my mind. I'm inclined to rush it, which is not my style. Perhaps the wine is doing this to me. I decide to take a step back and go downstairs for a snack. If I don't eat something soon, I'm going to be drunk off my ass by dinner time.

Stepping back from the piece, I cannot help but smile. I've outdone myself this afternoon. I quickly clean my hands and wrap the sculpture snugly in a plastic wrap to keep it moist. I toss my apron on my chair, pull the elastic band from my hair, and stroke my fingers through the strands.

While I descend the stairs, I hear Carl talking to another man. Who on earth would be visiting him in the middle of the day? When I reach the last stair, I peer around the corner to the kitchen and see the backside of a man I don't recognize. When I enter the room, I clear my throat to catch their attention. "What's going on, Carl?" I ask.

The man Carl is talking to turns his head, and we lock eyes. Immediately I feel unsettled. His smile widens. It lights up his entire face, and I cannot help but smile back.

"Hi. I'm Olivia," I say, offering my hand to him.

Carl gives me a stern look as if I'm interrupting one of his classes. I try to ignore him, but it is impossible to do that. "Go back to your studio, Olivia. I can handle this." Carl bites out.

My back gets up instantly. "Handle what, exactly, Carl?" The young man stuck between us tries not look lost, but we are making him rather uncomfortable. I relax a bit when I realize fighting with Carl in front of this stranger is bad manners.

Carl's stern eyes remain fixed on mine. "What is the purpose of your visit?" I ask, trying to break the tension in the room. I notice a set of documents upon the kitchen table and step forward to review them. Shock runs through me. "Are you trying to sell the apartment, Carl?" I raise my eyes to him and give him my version of the teacher's not happy look.

"We're divorcing, Olivia. I want what is mine, and the only way to get that is to sell. Surely you didn't think you'd keep it and toss me out," he states as he folds his arms across his chest.

"Well, Carl. It would have been nice of you to include me in this plan. How do you know I wasn't going to buy you out for the value portion that is yours? Do you even consider me for one minute of the day?" I cannot help my tone or the anger welling inside of me. I'm furious that I have to bring this conversation to the forefront in strange company. I flick my gaze to the young man who has yet to utter his name to me and try to muster a polite smile. "I'm sorry. What did you say your name was?"

Before he can answer, I state firmly, "I have no interest in selling this apartment. Would you mind leaving the documents and letting us contact you later?"

61

He smiles nervously and nods. "My name is Clint McPhee, and I'd be happy to discuss this with you both at another time. Please let me know your decision when you've finalized your plans."
Without another word, Clint swiftly exits the apartment. I sit my ass down in the nearest chair and begin reviewing the realty papers Clint left behind. I notice the name of the real estate agency, Max Donovan Realty, and the coincidence surprises me.

Carl is still standing in the middle of the kitchen with his arms folded. "Well, you really do know how to put on a show, Olivia. That was rude and uncalled for."

"Rude and uncalled for?" I laugh and shake my head. "You do not own this apartment. *We* own this apartment. What gave you the idea that you could put my home up for sale without discussing it with me first?"

Carl doesn't answer me. Instead, he marches out of the kitchen like a scolded teenager and heads to his den to hide. As he storms off, I call out to him, "This is not the last of this conversation, Carl."

Chapter 12 – Max

The news from Clint about the kitchen incident at Olivia's house bothered me. Even if I didn't have a connection to the clients, this is one of those situations which I can attest to having been in the middle of multiple times, and it is always ugly. Perhaps I should have delivered the listing papers directly, but I was shy on time this week. I pick up my phone off my desk and start dialing Olivia's number. I hope that she answers and that the argument between her and her husband didn't escalate after Clint left. Two rings, three rings, six rings later, and my call goes to voicemail. Dammit! My message is brief and on task before I hang up.

I huff out a frustrated breath and toss my phone atop my desk. Once again, my coffee has gone stone cold, and I may get a fresh one while figuring out how to deal with this situation. He wants to sell, she doesn't, and they have little to no communication skills to work with. I don't have much choice but to wait for Olivia to return my call and see how far the two of them got with listing the property.

It is well past five o'clock when Olivia returns my call. I try not to smile when I see her name appear on my phone screen since I know the conversation isn't going to be light, but the thought of talking to her excites me. "Hello, Olivia," I say, trying to be as business-like as possible.

"Hey, Max. When did Carl contact you about selling our apartment?"

"Just two days ago. I didn't make the connection to you and Carl as he never mentioned his last name when he booked the appointment with my office. He just said his name was Carl and gave us the address."

"Oh. That sounds like him. He never gives out his last name unless he's asked for it. Such a strange coincidence that he'd call your agency." A bit of silence hangs between us and I'm about to say something, but she jumps in ahead of my thoughts. "So, I guess you heard about poor Clint being stuck in the middle of Carl's attempt to sell our apartment out from underneath me."

"Yes. Don't worry about any of that or Clint for that matter. He's a big boy. What I want to know is how you are doing. I understand this is frustrating, and I want you to know I've seen this kind of situation arise more often than you'd imagine." I'm hoping my compassion for her dilemma calms her. I can hear a number of my staff getting ready to head home for the night, and I rise to close my office door for privacy and to block out the ruckus. Tucking my phone between my chin and shoulder, I pull out a notepad and start writing down ideas on how to salvage a possible sale and make sure Olivia has a perfect replacement home for herself if that is what she and Carl decide to do.

As much as my business mind is rolling out ideas, my endgame is to make her happy. I have to ask her a few questions to see if my thoughts are worth presenting to her and Carl. "So, we are clear on the fact that Carl wants to sell, and you do not. Is it the shock of his actions of hiring a realtor without discussing it with you that makes you upset or that you might lose your home in the divorce?" I lean back in my chair and hold my breath. This could go either way.

"Max," (she says in a drawn-out breathy way.) "I've had a few hours to think this over, and I need to make a couple of phone calls before deciding what course of action is best. I shouldn't be shocked that Carl would pull something like this because he's not in his right mind. However, if I can't secure the funds I need to buy him out and kick his non-communicative ass out the door, then a sale is inevitable. The thought of me becoming homeless is unsettling, to say the least. I've never not had a home or a place to create my art. I want to cry, but I'm too angry for that."

I lean forward and place my elbows on the desk surface, pondering my best response. "You won't be homeless. That I can promise you, Olivia. Please don't let that worry you. If you decide to sell the apartment, we can add a clause to whichever property you offer on for yourself, stating that it is subject to your current apartment's sale if your home hasn't sold before you find a good replacement. There are other ways to deal with this situation, but this is the most common scenario." I begin tapping a pen on the desk, flipping it end over end, tip to tail nervously. I'm worried that I'm upsetting her more, and that is what I had hoped to avoid during this conversation.

"Okay. I understand. I have options, and that's good to know. My biggest worry is always about where I'd have a studio. I'd rather die than give up creating sculptures." I hear another long breath from her through the receiver, and I grimace.

"Can I meet you for coffee, lunch, or dinner somewhere tomorrow? I'd like to help you as best I can, and it would be much easier to do this face to face." My thoughts came out a little quicker than I'd planned. Part of me wants to help her, and the other part of me is still dying to meet her. I could kill two birds with one stone. The sale is far less important than meeting Olivia, but I'd rather dress up my suggestion as a business transaction than let her know how anxious I am to be in her presence, finally.

I begin clicking my pen open and shut with the tip of my thumb while waiting for her to decide if even sharing a coffee somewhere would suit her. I stop clicking and close my eyes.

"Yes. Lunch tomorrow? Can you fit that in your schedule?" she asks, and I do a fist pump and silently yell yes.

In a perfectly calm voice, I reply, "Excellent. I'll pick you up at your apartment at eleven-thirty. I have the perfect place to enjoy lunch and talk business." I stand in front of my desk and pace a little while she confirms it's okay to pick her up. I get the yes I need and wonder if I should keep her talking or let her go. She sighs again, then asks me, "How was your day?"

I'm a bit shocked, but that subsides nearly instantly when it's replaced with a big assed grin. "It was fine. Thanks for asking. I noticed during my tour of your apartment that you are working on a new sculpture. Do you care to let me in on what you are creating?"

"Hmm. I like to keep my projects secret and then do a public reveal only when it's finished. I think I can trust you to keep my secrets so I'll give you a hint. I like to work with natural subjects. This time around, I'm crafting something ocean-related. What do you suppose I'm creating?"

My pacing before my desk stops, and I want to sit somewhere that will allow me to kick up my feet. I turn my two client chairs to face each other, sit in one, and rest my feet on the other's seat. My tie gets a good tug to loosen it and I roll my sleeve up on both arms. While I fidget to get comfortable, I ponder Olivia's question. The first thing that comes to mind is something big like a whale, dolphin, or octopus, which are common sculpture subjects.

"Is it a mammal?"

"No," she replies. I can hear a smile in her voice, even with that one simple word reply. This is good. I want her to smile.

"A crustacean?"

"Nope. Try again."

This time I hear a bit of a giggle. She's enjoying the guessing game, and that puts another huge-assed smile on my face. "Then it must be an invertebrate," I say, feeling like my guess is as solid as it's ever going to be. What else is there in the ocean that she could craft from clay?

"Nice try. You've done a great job of the process of elimination, but you are missing the obvious."

"Am I now. How interesting. What would be obvious that I'm overlooking?" (I say in a bit of a lower tone.) She has me stumped. I don't want to sound stupid, but I really have no idea what else there is in the ocean besides mammals, crustaceans, and invertebrates.

"Do you give up?" she asks and giggles again. The sound of her laughter is music to my ears. I could listen to that sound all day long. Then it dawns on me. Sound – repetition - ocean. "You are creating a wave?"

"Yes! I found an old photograph of a wave I shot in Cancun years ago. It looked like it was in the midst of a dance like two people were reaching out their hands to one another to begin a baile folklorico."

(I chuckle). "What is a baile folklorico? Did I pronounce that right?"

"Ooh, I get to educate you this evening. How exciting! It is a broad term for Mexican folk dancing, encompassing several styles of dances."

My smile widens, and I nod in acceptance that she is much smarter than I am. "If we were talking about the culture of New York, I'd be all there, but anything outside of my city and I'm kind of a dumb ass." (chuckle). I'm being modest, but I want to make her laugh again.

"I highly doubt you could be considered a dumb ass, Max."

"You're right. I'm a card-carrying member of Mensa, but I don't like to boast about it. What is your IQ? Or have you never been tested?"

A burst of riotous and nearly ear-splitting laughter comes

through my phone. I laugh with her even though I have no idea what she found so amusing in my last question. "I'd venture to say most artists have low IQ's, and although I've never been officially tested, I'm going to say it's around 65." She snickers and then snort laughs, and that just makes me laugh harder. She's lying about artists being stupid, but I enjoy her attempt at a wisecrack.

"Yeah, me too. Mensa actually has an auto-renewable restraining order out on me because I tried to join them too many times."

"That is too funny, Max. You have a great sense of humor. I like that. It's the best quality any human can have. Laughter heals all, you know?" I'm smiling from ear to ear now, and for some odd reason, my face is hot. She's hot. I don't fucking care what she looks like anymore. This woman has stolen my heart from the total sum of two telephone conversations. How hard up do I have to be having this kind of reaction? I give my head a shake and sigh. "Listen, Olivia. I should let you go. We can continue to insult ourselves for entertainment value tomorrow at lunch."

"You're right. We shouldn't waste all our good jokes over the phone. I'm excited to meet with you tomorrow. After these conversations, it will be great to meet you face to face."

"Yes, I agree," I say, as I try yet again to envision her. Brunette? Blonde? Redhead? Tall? Short? Shit. If all my dreams are about to unfold, Olivia will not only be the amazingly talented woman I've come to secretly lust after but be the vision of beauty I can only hope for. Tomorrow can't come soon enough.

Chapter 13 – Olivia

While I should have spent the better part of my morning doing some housework, I was still too pissed off at Carl to feel obligated to clean up after him. He can clean his bathroom and all the newspapers lying in a pile on the floor by his favourite chair. I'm not his maid anymore. And while I think of it, I'll make him a note to tell him he can get his own groceries from the store and feed himself. All bets are off.

I wander the apartment aimlessly while Carl still sleeps. The memories here flood back to me as I pick up photographs from the side tables of our various travels. It dawns on me that we've only the one photo of the two of us in Carl's den hidden among his countless books on the shelves. Is that weird? This apartment has been my haven for fifteen years, and I don't know that I'm as ready to sell it as Carl is. But I must keep my mind open. Do I really want to stay here without Carl and relive our past life together every day, or do I want to start fresh with new surroundings that I can call my own?

So many decisions. I hope Max has the answers I need when we talk at lunch today. I've not been out to lunch with anyone, friend, or business acquaintance for a while. I can't decide how fancy I need to dress as Max didn't tell me the name of the place he was taking me. I'll have to pick something business casual so as not to be underdressed for the restaurant. A white pencil skirt and my baby blue sleeveless silk button-up blouse will keep me cool in the heat and be presentable in any situation. And I'm going to assume Max is wearing a suit since this is a business meeting. The only thing I have left to do before I head out is to apply lipstick. Just as I've opened the tube, my cell phone rings out from the edge of my bed. Reaching for it, I see it is Max calling. "Good morning, Max. Are you here now?" I ask.

The Art of Love in New York City

"Good morning, Olivia. Should I come upstairs to get you, or would you rather meet me outside?"

"I'll come down. Just five minutes, alright?

"Yes. My driver and I are ready when you are. Take your time."

After I hang up my phone, I feel a flush of heat coat my skin. Oh, this is not good. It's hot as bloody hell already out there. If I'm getting hot flashes...no wait. I'm not old enough for fucking hot flashes. What the hell then? I must be more nervous than I thought I was. I dab my brow with a tissue from the vanity counter and apply my lipstick. I take a good long look at myself in the mirror and smile. "Every day is a new day. Go out and do it right," I say to my reflection.

Chapter 14 – Max

I debated on whether to remove my jacket or not, but this ninety-degree heat is unbearable in a full suit. I remove the jacket and drape it casually over my arm, fold my arms across my chest and lean against my car while I wait for Olivia.

A lovely and leggy brunette approaches the front doors to the building, and my heart pumps a little faster. Is that her? Not too shabby. I don't mind brunettes. The approaching woman strides like she's on a mission through the lobby of the building and waits for the automatic doors to open for her. I ease my body off the car and stand erect, smiling like a fool at this woman exiting the building. When she's through the doors, she sees me smiling at her, and I hold my hand up to wave, so she knows who to look for. The woman smiles cautiously, returns my wave, and then continues her determined stride west down the sidewalk.

I just made a fool of myself to a perfect stranger. I can't help but chuckle, give my head a shake and lean my ass against my car again. It is a good thing Harjit is in the driver's seat so she didn't see me do that. She'd have been laughing at that for days. As I'm shaking my head and looking down at the curb I'm standing on, I hear my name called out.

"Max?"

My head jolts up, and I smile wide, knowing that voice only too well. "Olivia. So nice to finally meet you in person," I'm not sure if those were the right words or not. They seemed a bit formal, considering she and I have been subtly seducing each other over the phone and through texts. She's a shapely and surprisingly attractive woman and that suits me just fine. Flaxen hair flows over her shoulders in a soft wave, and bright blue eyes that contain just a

71

smidge of sorrow in them lock on mine while she comes to halt before me.

I have to remind myself that this is a delicate situation. Our lunch date is supposed to be a business meeting, but at the same time, I'm trying to be casual Max – the guy she knows and has flirted with on the phone, not the realtor that is helping her decide to market her home.

A bright smile comes my way, with her hand out to shake mine. Okay, that makes sense. She's taking this to a more formal level today, and I can work with that. I shake her hand and stare her in the eyes. She does the same. As we stare, our hands stay clasped together. In a feminine gesture, she cups her other hand over mine and gives it a gentle squeeze then slowly slides her fingers free from this physical connection.

A feather's touch – elegant, sensual – my smile hardens as does my cock. She's more beautiful than I expected. But what did I expect? I had some ideas in my head about what she may look like, and I'm reminded of the internal questions that filled my head last night after our phone call. Setting aside all the things I wondered about her appearance, I could not be happier to meet her finally.

"What is the name of the restaurant you chose? Have I dressed appropriately?"

I nod and can't wipe the god damned smile off my face. "Perry's Boathouse. And your attire is perfect." I want to tell her *she* is perfect, but that might be pushing the boundaries.

I manage to get her to laugh for me on our drive to the restaurant. I wanted to see her face when she laughed, and I was not disappointed. She goes a little pink and holds her hand under her nose, which was an unexpected turn on. She has a free spirit that feels like it has been contained for too long. Is that what marriage does to people? I've never married, but if she continues to be this delicious, I may reconsider my position on that subject. I remind myself to stop moving so far ahead in the future with my thoughts and focus on the here and now. We arrive at our destination, and Harjit opens the car door for Olivia as I climb out the other side. She thanks Harjit as I join them on the sidewalk.

"I have no idea how long this meeting will run, Harjit. Do whatever you want for the time being, and I'll call you when we're ready to be picked up. A couple of hours at least."

Our server seats us next to the window at a table for two. It's intimate, and the view is amazing. If we run out of things to say, we can always look out the window, and I can't tell you how many times that has happened with awkward client meetings. I use this table frequently.

I'm a little lost for words as I watch her every move. I'm not sure how to start this conversation and decide that I'll go the business route first. If she wants to get casual later, and I hope she does, I'm happy to accommodate her. "What would make you stay at your apartment, assuming money is no issue?"

Her bright blue eyes rise to meet mine over her menu in her hands, and I try not to smile like a fool.

"I thought about that this morning. We've been there for fifteen years, and so I have a lot of good memories. It is only since Carl's stroke that the apartment has felt, I don't know, not like a home. But I love my studio space more than anything, and that is what has me so concerned. It makes me very anxious to think that I'd not find any other space to compare," she admits.

I nod and fully understand. People often find change, especially drastic ones, difficult to envision. Change is hard under most circumstances, and fifteen years is a long time to get attached to a living space. "Are you worried that you won't be able to buy out

73

Carl's half of the apartment?"

"Yes. My father has always helped me out when I needed it, but there was no need to bother him for financial assistance after I married Carl. I may have to bite the bullet and reach out to him. It would be an investment for dad as a joint owner, so I think I could persuade him to help me. There is no mortgage as we paid that off two years ago."

"You are in a better situation than most. It is rare to meet people who don't have a mortgage outstanding." I don't understand why they don't make the two apartments separate again, and each live where they are, but maybe that hasn't crossed their minds as the most obvious solution to their situation.

"Yes, I suppose you're right."

Our server returns to take our drink orders, our meal orders, and fill our water glasses. Our conversation becomes easy once the meals arrive as I see her relax a bit more when she has something to occupy her hands while we talk. I mention that I have a loft that she should look at if she decides to sell their apartment. The price is a little higher than I'd like it to be, but the client is firm on the higher asking price. And the listing is only a few blocks west of Olivia's current apartment.

I pose my question between bites of my baked salmon meal. "Would you be free after lunch to have a quick peek at a loft space I have a listing on? I want to show you that there are places available where an artist studio would be perfect."

Olivia takes a sip of her wine and gently places it down on the table. Her eyes fix on mine, and a slow smile comes my way.

"I'll entertain the idea. If you think it would be a good replacement for my current studio, then I'm open to having a peek."

"Perfect. I don't want to press you. I just want you to know you have options. Good options."

"Okay. I'm game. Is there a specific time you had an appointment made for the showing?"

"We can go as soon as we're done here. The loft is empty."

As with our telephone and texting conversations, we find ourselves comfortable in each other's company during this lunch meeting. I smile as I dig out my credit card to pay for our meals. "Did you enjoy your lunch?" I ask, and our eyes connect again. That smile of hers comes back, and she nods.

"Delicious. Thank you."

No, sweetheart, you are the delicious one. "Glad to hear it." I gesture with my hand for Olivia to take the lead to exit as I text Harjit to see if she's nearby to pick us up. She replies that she's outside in the parkade. I swear Harjit has a sixth sense for when I need her.

I pose my question about dividing the two apartments, and she shakes her head at me.

"It would cost thousands of dollars to make those changes as the upper unit has no kitchen. It would make perfect sense for us to do that, but I don't have the money for major renovations, and Carl isn't interested to do the work. It is better to sell it as is and move on."

We reach the loft apartment within twenty minutes. No street parking is available, and so we are dropped off in front of the building. We take the private elevator to the sixth floor, and it opens directly into the loft. I watch Olivia to see her reaction to how this loft is accessed as it isn't common to open an elevator door directly into a private living space. She appears to love it. "What is your first impression?"

The Art of Love in New York City

"Wow! That's really something. I've never seen this private elevator thing when you land right inside your apartment before. It's very New York chic," I love that she's already impressed. Hopefully, she finds the openness of the space equally as appealing. So far, this is a win.

As she slowly soaks in the high ceilings, the large picture windows and the light streaming in from the south-facing view, her smile once again lights up her pretty features. I point over to the far left of the elevator and mention that I thought the light from the windows would be perfect for a workspace. She agrees and walks over to that corner, spins slowly as if she is picturing in her head where she'd put an easel for her paintings and where she'd set up a table for her sculpture work.

There are a few upper cabinets affixed to the wall adjacent to the windows that she could use to store various art supplies. It is almost perfect. "It is a wonderful space, Max. It's like you read my mind. There are a few things that I'd add or change, but overall this is truly impressive."

"Come. Let me show you the bedroom space and the bathroom. It has been recently renovated so there would be nothing to do there. The only problem I see in this loft is that it's a one-bedroom unit. I think that is the reason it hasn't sold."

"One bedroom suits me fine, Max. Carl and I never had children, so I don't need extra space for sleeping." Olivia sighs as she enters the bedroom, but in a good way, not a sad sigh. "I love this!" she says as she wanders over toward the bedroom window, which is nearly the wall's full height and almost as wide.

"It has an electric blind system that you can operate from either a wall switch or a handheld controller," I point out, which makes her smile wider.

"You sure know how to show a client a good time," she teases and laughs. "This loft is absolutely amazing. Is this the top floor?"

"Yes. There is access to the roof from a side door next to the kitchen. I'll show it to you later. Perfect for stargazing on warm summer nights," I add and wink at her.

She goes back to appreciating the view and privacy aspect from the window. I walk toward her where she stands. This window's angle and the fact that the other building next to it is shorter than this sixth-floor loft means that the blinds don't need to be closed for privacy. For a bedroom in New York City, that is a major selling point.

I find myself standing a bit closer behind her than I should. The scent of her hair and the subtle perfume she wears infiltrates my senses. I have this undeniable urge to wrap my arms around her from behind and nest my chin on her shoulder, holding her close to my chest. I need to step away before I act on my desires.

Just as I'm about to step back, Olivia turns her head and locks her eyes on mine. We stare at each other silently, searching deep into each other's souls. What the hell is this woman doing to me? That look is killing any resolve I had to keep my hands off her. Without even thinking about it my left arm gently wraps around her waist, and in the same instant, she leans forward and kisses me. One kiss. Why did she do that? I'm instantly rock hard for her, and I'm not the kind of guy that slows down when things turn hot. I want her like I've never wanted anyone before her. Does she sense this? Is that why she kissed me?

Another long stare between us makes me wonder what is going on inside that beautiful head of hers. Fuck this. I'm going in for another taste of her, and I hope like hell she isn't playing games with my head. Her eyes soften, and I take my chance. My arm grips her waist a little tighter, and I plant my lips on hers with full intention. Not a peck, not a tease, a full-on heady kiss that I both want and need from her.

The Art of Love in New York City

She falls into me as she turns her body to be embraced. I feel her slip her arms around my hips and press herself firmly against me. She's not turning me down, and I'm not stopping this freight train's worth of need coursing through my veins.

I reach up to hold her face in my hands. I'm ready for whatever comes next, and she needs to know I'm all in. Our tongues tangle, the kisses deepen, the breathing pace quickens, and I'm hard as steel.

I pause for a second to look at her directly again. She searches mine, licks her lips, and then begins to undo my belt buckle and pants button.

"Are you sure?" I ask, my voice low and filled with intent.

Olivia nods before diving into my face for more lust-filled kisses. Seconds later, my pants drop to my feet, but I'm not letting her disrobe me before I get the chance to pull her blouse over her head and feel those incredible tits of hers. The low-cut V of her baby blue blouse had me testing my willpower to keep my eyes on her face throughout lunch, and now I need to feel them in my greedy palms.

She laughs lightly, and that smile of hers chances an appearance as I let her blouse slip from my fingers to the floor. I hold her around her curvy frame while my hands appreciate the softness of her skin. I find the clasp of her bra across her back and undo the hooks without hesitation.

Her breaths come faster now between our kisses while I slide her bra off her shoulders. She's a bit anxious, nervous perhaps but not wavering from this dance we're in. We continue to remove one piece of clothing at a time as quickly as we can until I realize I've still got my shoes on. I kick them off, and in doing so, I'm now eye to eye with her. She's still standing in her heels, and as far as I'm concerned, she can leave them on.

I knead her left breast while my right hand slips between her silky soft skin and her panties. She's hot, wet and I need to be inside of her as soon as possible. "I want to taste you," I murmur in her ear.

"Please," she begs. I kiss her sweetly and lower myself to my knees. Her hands run in gentle strokes through my hair while I slip off her panties and tuck my face between her legs. Her naked body is pressed up against the glass window while I lick and suck at her, tasting the sweet wetness that is there because of her desire for me. We are drunk on each other, and as much as I'd like to blame the wine at lunch, I know this is raw need and an instant connection that is driving us to this place in time.

A soft moan escapes her lips while my cock grows harder for her with every second she lets me be with her like this. I hold my hands firmly around the back of her thighs, and she spreads her legs a little wider for me. Reaching up with one hand, I cup her breast while I intensify my teasing of her clit. I need her to come for me like this. I want her satisfied before I fill her. To me, she deserves to be given all the sexual bliss she can handle.

To increase the level of pleasure I'm giving her, I slide my other hand between her legs and pump two fingers inside of her while I gently suck on her sweet pussy. Her breath hitches and a little whimper escapes her lips before her legs go rigid, and I know she's about to arrive. When she reaches her peak, it is glorious, dangerous, sexy as fuck, and I watch her face closely as she comes.

I rise to my feet and hold her steady as she calms down from her orgasmic high. Her eyes open for a second, and then she closes them again. You have no idea how good you taste," I murmur then dive into her for a sensual sharing of her bounty. I kiss her tenderly, as I worry I'm taking more than my welcome, but then she grips me in her delicate hands and begins long, firm strokes of my rigid cock.

It is my turn to moan against her lips, and she knows she's got me right where she wants me – crazy in the head, seduced and ready to blow in her hands if she doesn't stop the stroking and massaging of my crown with her palm.

"I need to fuck you, Olivia. Don't make me come like this. I want to be inside you when I come," I say as I bite her lip and tug.

She slows her teasing of me by gently rubbing the pre-cum over my crown. She leans down between our bodies and licks it off me, whirling her tongue in circles, sucking only hard enough to make me want to say her name in the form of a beg. My hands press hard against the window behind her as my eyes chinch shut at the glory of this moment. She needs to stop what she's doing to me before I lose it in her mouth.

Olivia senses my limits. She rises, wraps her arms around my neck and smiles at me. She raises her right leg over my hip, and I lift her into my arms. I walk us over to the opposing wall, pressing her back against the cold concrete surface, and sink myself inside of her nice and slow. I want to be looking into her eyes as we fuck each other. I want her to know how much this means to me and that she is important. This is not a quick fuck. This is me finally getting off on a woman that has had me by the balls for the past few weeks.

Our audible breaths match each other as I drive into her pump after pump. Olivia smiles down on me, her eyes sparkle, her lips wet and so tempting. I kiss her while the last few pumps into her tight pussy send me over the edge. I come hard, and it seems to have drained every ounce of energy from me. "Do you have any idea how amazed I am of you?" I mean every word, and I can only hope she understands how much I needed this. How much I needed her.

Olivia rests her forehead against mine, rolls it slowly back and forth before I let her ease herself to the floor to her feet. We hug tight, chests still heaving slightly from the experience, skin on skin, without a care in the world. I close my eyes and kiss her sweet lips. What we did for each other was unplanned, beautiful, powerful, intense. "Are you cold?"

She eases her body away from mine with a light laugh, and her soft smile shines back at me. "No, but I suppose we shouldn't stand naked beside this window much longer." I nod and release her only long enough to gather our clothes from the floor. She takes her garments and kisses my shoulder. Taking my hand, she leads me into the bathroom to redress.

"Dare I inquire as to how much the seller is asking for the loft since we've already christened it?" A smirk forms over her pretty lips, and I cannot help but chuckle. I may even be blushing, just a little.

"We'll make the numbers work, Olivia. If you love it, you can have it." As she stands before the mirror, I see something in her that she likely doesn't see of herself. "Stay there just like that," I urge. I locate my cell phone in an attempt to capture her beauty in the light of the room. She only has her bra and panties on so far, but she looks amazing. When I snap the picture of her she laughs and tucks her hand under her nose again. It is the quintessential essence of who she is. Perfection. I'm so fucked. In her presence, I feel a high like no other.

Dare I admit to myself that Max has a stronghold on me that I never expected. Never have I let myself be so vulnerable to a man as I did yesterday in the loft. What was I thinking by letting myself be overcome with desire in such an unlikely space? But he truly blew me away. It was hot, dangerous, careless even, but somehow, I needed that more than I realized. It wasn't until he stood behind me, draped his strong arm around my waist that the urges took over complete control of me. I had to taste him. I had to have him if he was willing to partake. The memory of his lips on mine lingers even now, hours later. We were hungry and passionate, and I didn't expect that regardless of how I felt about him at that moment. Did he feel the same way for me? Was it an act, or was there really that strong of a connection between us?

I shake my head and try to press the memory of his touch and his mouth on me away. I need to focus on the here and now. I've been ignoring my sculpture of the wave for too long.

I regret this as I climb out of my bed and wander down the hall to my studio to check it. I should have done this yesterday when I returned home from my lunch with Max, but Carl and I had another heated argument, and I left to go for a run in the insipid afternoon heat to escape him. The run may have cleared my head a little, but it did something else. It made me realize that regardless of our impending divorce, I cheated on Carl twice now. Once with Teddy and now with Max, albeit neither encounter was premeditated. The word cheater repeats in my head like a scolding.

The reminder angers me while I slowly unwrap the plastic off my half-completed wave sculpture and realize that I'd not properly secured the plastic wrap. When I test the moisture content of the clay, I am angered even more. It is ruined. It is a glaring reminder that my perfect little life as I know it is destroyed.

The anger inside me for all the things out of my control that has transpired come to a head as I growl low in my throat and smash my hand down atop the clay. I punch the sculpture three more times before I'm satisfied that I've destroyed it. I realize it was a childish reaction, but it felt good to get mad, lash out, and feel something. This is the one thing that I never allowed myself to do after Carl's stroke. I never got angry or figured out that I needed to get angry. I'm reminded that these changes in Carl are a kind of death to me, an end to our relationship, and all the years we made together as two halves of a whole. The question now is, what is going to happen next?

Still charged with a passion for resolving my current situation with Carl, I storm my way downstairs, past the kitchen, and bust through Carl's bedroom door, ready to give him a piece of my mind that I'd not yet shared with him. I'm mad that our sex life is non-existent, mad that the man I devoted my life to has changed so dramatically that I don't even recognize him as my husband, and mad that he wants to divorce me when I should be the one divorcing him.

The door flings open and slams against the wall beside it startling both of us. But that isn't the only startle in store for me. Carl is on the edge of his bed in the full throws of masturbating while videotaping his actions on his cell phone. What the fresh hell is this? He's never masturbated in front of me, but he's willingly videoing this incredibly personal act on his phone. Who is he making the video for? Has he been cheating on me with someone else?

"Carl!"

My blood boils inside me as I turn on my heels and storm back up to my bedroom. I want to cry, but I'm too frustrated and shocked to do that. Now it all makes sense. He's been having an affair with someone online while I dutifully catered to his every need, hoping that someday we'd be back to who we were. I gave him nearly a year, and he ignored me the entire time. It was all for not.

The Art of Love in New York City

My earlier self-loathing for having cheated on Carl with Teddy and Max emotionally and physically is long gone. It is laughable. As much as I tried to communicate with Carl about my feelings of devotion and my need to have him touch me the way he used to, I now see that it would never happen. I'd lost Carl long ago. And I wonder if he has been having this affair since before his stroke. So many questions are unanswered. If I'm honest with myself, I don't want to know the answers anymore. Fuck it all. We're done as husband and wife. That is written in stone.

My first impulse is to phone Max and tell him about my morning, but I think Sasha is the only person I'll call today. She'll understand, be on my side and nurture me in my time of emotional turmoil. I find my phone connected to the charger on my dresser and unplug it. Sasha should be on her way to the gallery at this time of the morning, and so I can have this conversation with her while she drives.

Just as I'm dialing her number, my phone pings, and a text message from Max pops up in a notification on my screen. I take a few steps backward to sit at the edge of my bed. Should I answer him or ignore it?

Max: "Good morning, beautiful."

I drop my phone beside me on the bed and begin to massage my temples. I mumble aloud, "No, Max. It is not a good morning. It is in fact, the shittiest morning I've lived in my entire life." I huff out an exaggerated breath and pick my phone back up. I reread his message and decide to text him back.

Me: "Good morning, Max."

My fingers hover over the keypad while I think of something more to add. But I'm drawing a blank. I send this simple reply and wait.

Max: "Can I see you sometime today? Lunch?"

Me: "I haven't organized my day yet. Can I get back to you on lunch?"

Max: "Yes. But don't make me wait too long. I need to see you."

"Well, at least somebody loves me," I mumble. The image of Max and I making love inside the empty loft space fills my head again, and my heart begins to pump faster. My anger has subsided, replaced with an uncontrollable smile. That was the most amazing sex I've ever had. It was foolish of me to let myself be made love to by a man I barely know, but so good I can't stop thinking about it. He understands my needs better than I do. He played my body for everything it was worth, and I'd do it again in an instant.

Me: Okay. Lunch is good. Where should I meet you?"

Max and I make our lunch arrangements, and I decide not to call Sasha. Why ruin her day with my problems? They won't go away by talking about it as I've already attempted that approach with Carl. I would far rather focus on Max and what our lunch date.

I'm seated in the center of the bistro while my server attempts to find me a table on the sidewalk under the canape. It's crazy hot outside, but this location is perfect and romantic. I hope Olivia loves this place as much as I do.

I text Olivia to tell her I'm inside waiting for her. Within a few minutes, I see her gorgeous face, body, and smile as she enters through the front doors. I could never get enough of seeing her like this.

As she approaches, I reach for her and give her the kiss I've been dying to plant on her perfect lips since I woke this morning. "You are a vision - a dream. Tell me I'm not dreaming, Olivia," I murmur in her ear.

I lean back and watch a pretty flush of pink skate across her face, and I know my work is done here. "Sit," I say, pointing at the open chair beside me. "I'm waiting on a table for us outside. Is that alright?"

"Yes. As long as we are in the shade, it should be good."

Her smile lights up my entire being, and I know I'm crushing hard for her. "Did you manage to work a little more on your wave sculpture? I'm interested to see it completed."

Olivia laughs, perhaps a bit harder than I expected. "Oh, I worked on it alright," she says as her laughter subsides. "It's gone, Max. I destroyed it this morning in a childish fit of anger. I'll have to approach the idea of the wave later when my life is less disjointed."

Our server approaches to tell us she has an available table, and we follow her to the patio. I pull out Olivia's chair for her to sit down and then sit across from her at the small round table. After our menus are placed in our hands, our water glasses get filled to the rim. I nod at our server as Olivia and I review the single-paged, board wrapped menu. She remains quiet as she decides on what to order.

I've been here enough to know what the menu has to offer, so I wait for her to choose. "Everything here is good," I mention, and she nods at me. "You seem a bit off today. Is everything alright?"

"Yes. Well, mostly. I'm pissed about a few things, nothing of which has anything to do with you, Max. She leans forward to whisper to me. "I found Carl videoing himself masturbating. I was shocked, as you can well imagine, and now I have to assume he's having an affair with someone online."

My eyes bulge a little at her confession, but I don't want to make a big deal of it. "Are you sure about the online affair, or are you guessing?"

"Fuck, I don't know. But why else would he be videoing that act? He's certainly not sending that bit of footage to my cell phone! No, no, no," she says, wagging her finger in front of her face. "In all the years we've been together, he never once did that act for me or asked me to do it for him to watch. He's definitely sending it to someone else." Olivia huffs out a quick breath, and a few strands of her hair dance along her forehead.

"I'm sorry, Olivia. I can't imagine how it would feel to see that knowing it wasn't intended for you."

Olivia leans forward again to speak quietly to me. "Hey. You know what? I don't care. He's asked me for a divorce, and he can have it without question. Especially now. I woke up this morning feeling incredibly guilty for what you and I shared yesterday. Carl and I are still married, and until the divorce is finalized, I technically cheated on him."

The Art of Love in New York City

I sip my water while I try to think of something to say. Maybe I should just nod and let the conversation slip away for the time being. As I look out toward the patio section behind Olivia's shoulder, I nearly choke on my sip of water as I see my ex-fiancé approaching me. *Goddammit. Why the fuck is she here now?*

Kelsey struts toward the café entry doors, and as much as I tried to hide myself, I am spotted. A devilish grin comes my way, and I utter under my breath, "Here we go." Olivia turns her head to see what has caught my attention and watches as Kelsey approaches our table.

"Hello, Max," she says in a low tone. "Entertaining a client today, or is this a *friend* of yours that I haven't met?" I know exactly what the emphasis on friend meant, and my back gets up instantly. My smile is as fake as Kelsey is as I introduce Olivia as a client. Olivia reaches her hand out to shake Kelsey's, and I internally groan while my fake smile remains fixed on my face.

"Nice to meet you, Olivia. If you find that Max isn't producing the real estate results you need, please don't hesitate to contact me," she coos as she pulls her business card out of her purse and hands it to Olivia.

I shake my head in disbelief and chuckle. "That isn't how I taught you to gather new business, Kelsey. In fact, it is against the Real Estate Board of New York's code of ethics to poach existing clients from other realtors." My reprimand goes unnoticed by Kelsey as her eyes stay fixed on Olivia. After they exchange polite smiles, Kelsey's head turns slowly toward me, and she winks.

"I'm closing a six point eight million dollar deal this afternoon for Paul Quincy. Just another successful day at the office," she says in a sing-song way, being cocky.

"How many times did you have to suck him off before he agreed to let you sell his property?" I say under my breath but intending it to be just loud enough for Kelsey to hear. I get a stern look from Olivia, and I can't help but chuckle again. If Olivia only knew what Kelsey pulled on me two years ago, she'd not given me that look. She'd have laughed with me.

"Don't you think it's a tad unprofessional to speak to a fellow associate like that in front of your client?" Kelsey states, trying to make me look bad.

"Olivia is also a good friend. Run along now, Kelsey." I make a shooing gesture with my hand. "Let the grownups have their meal in peace," I say and wink back at her. Kelsey tries not to look pissed off, but I know her well enough to understand I've triggered a small war. She strides away as easily as she did when she arrived, and I'm happy to have her gone.

"Do you care to explain what that was all about?" Olivia asks, as her right brow pitches high at me, and her pretty lips press to a hard line. Our server comes to take our meal orders just then. We let the interruption cool the situation down a bit before I have to explain myself.

"Listen, Olivia. First, I apologize for talking to another woman like that in front of you. Second, Kelsey and I have a long history of stabbing each other in the back. She brings out the worst in me. Later I'll tell you about it, but for now, can we just enjoy this time together? I have a client meeting at the office at two o'clock that I cannot reschedule.

Olivia nods and sips her water while people who walk past the bistro's patio catch her attention. I'm mad at myself for letting Kelsey get under my skin so easily. She is the last person on this planet that I'd ever want to introduce to Olivia. This sits heavily in my heart like a bad omen. I give my head an imaginary shake and focus on the woman seated in front of me, who I can't get enough of.

89

The Art of Love in New York City

The balance of our meal and conversation is light, fun, and from time to time, we share a soul-searching look into each other's eyes from across the table. I wonder if Olivia realizes how much everything she does turns me on. I jacked off three times last night just thinking about her.

I insisted that Olivia have dinner with me tonight at my apartment. There is no way I'm letting her eat alone, and I need to hold her and kiss her again without any distractions or time limits. It has become difficult for me to focus on my work when she infiltrates virtually every space in my head and heart. How a woman, any woman, can have that much control baffles me.

I've tried to make my dining room look as romantic as I can. An interior decorator I am not, but I'm pleased with what I came up with.

I'm anxious. I don't entertain in my apartment often, but I'm fairly organized and tidy, considering how hectic my lifestyle is. Olivia arrives on time, and a three-tap knock on my door brings a smile to my face. I open the door slowly and lean my shoulder against the door jamb casually as I reach for her hands. "Welcome. Did you have any trouble finding the building or parking?"

"No, surprisingly. I got a spot out front, but I couldn't find a sign to indicate how many hours I was allowed to park there."

"Come in," I say and close the door behind her. She does a quick once over of the apartment with her eyes, then turns to me and smiles. "Give me your car keys. I'll move your car to the underground. My suite has two parking spaces, and I only use one of them. She nods and digs her keys out of her purse.

"It is the candy apple red Jaguar XJS. Do you like antique and collectible cars?"

"Sure, who doesn't appreciate an antique car in good

condition?"

"This one is fully restored. It was my dad's, and I took it off his hands two years ago. She's my baby, and she's very pretty," she says, dangling the keys in front of my face. I reach for them, and she snatches them away quickly.

"I promise to treat her with the utmost respect." I chuckle at her. I'm a bit surprised that she likes antique cars and that she's worried about me driving hers. I snag the keys away from her hand while I lean in for a kiss. There is so much we have to learn about each other. I slip the keys inside my pocket and let our lips linger just long enough to leave her wanting more. "I'll be back in ten minutes. Make yourself at home."

Chapter 17 – Olivia

As Max leaves to move my car, I walk over to his window to see if I can view him, but his living room faces the back of the building and not to the front where I parked. I'm sure he'll be okay to drive it. Why I'm so worried is beyond me, and I can only guess it is because I'm a little nervous about tonight. Since I have ten minutes to snoop, I begin by finding his bedroom and bathroom.

Nothing tells you more about a person than what their private space looks like. Down the hall behind the kitchen on the left is where the bedroom is – well, one of the bedrooms. I ease the half-open door fully and wander inside. The bed is made, the dirty laundry is in a basket next to the bathroom, not scattered all over the floor like I thought they might be. Peeking around the corner, I find his bathroom is equally as organized. I open a couple of drawers on the vanity and note he's definitely not a slob. I'm certain I'll discover something about Max that drives me crazy, but lack of cleanliness is not one of them.

I hear the sound of the apartment door opening, and I panic a little. I close the drawers and tiptoe quickly out of his room and pretend I was looking for his main bathroom. "Olivia?" he calls out.

"Yes. Sorry, I was looking for your bathroom. I went down the wrong hallway, I think."

"First door on your right," he calls back. I pretend to take a minute to pee and flush a perfectly clean toilet to legitimize my lie. I doubt he'd be happy about me snooping, but Max did say to make myself at home. That makes me giggle a bit. I run the tap water in the basin to complete my fake bathroom visit and exit with a big smile. "Your apartment is very nice, Max. How long have you been here?"

"Three years this September. Can I get you a glass of wine or something else to drink?"

"Wine, please," I say and walk toward him, where he's retrieving two wine glasses from a cabinet in his dining room. He holds the two glasses between his fingers by the stems at his side, and the sexiest smile emerges on his face.

"You really don't have any idea how beautiful you are, do you?" Max leans forward and kisses me sweetly. I want more of his mouth on mine, and the wine can wait. I hold his face close to mine with my hand behind his head to get another kiss. The only thing that is going to take my stress away is his hands on my body, his lips on my lips, his hard cock in my hand, and him begging me to let him fuck me. I instigated the first time we made love, and I'll do it again if he's worried about moving in on me sexually tonight.

"Olivia," he says between kisses. "Are we going to fuck each other senseless before or after the wine and dinner?"

"I'm ready when you are. Just say the word, Max," I whisper.

"I'm a lot hungrier for you than I am for fettuccini alfredo. Let me show you where I lay when I dream of you." My heart beats a little faster, and my clit begins to throb lightly. I don't know if he read that quote in a book somewhere, or it slipped out his mouth like he were Romeo, but that totally made me hot.

Max sets the two wine glasses on the dining room table then wraps his warm arms around my shoulders. I tuck my hands around his waist and look up at his handsome face. "I don't know exactly what it is that we're doing, Max, but I can't stop thinking about you, wanting you to touch me, kiss me. You control so many of my daily thoughts. Are you doing the same with thoughts of me?"

A broad smile forms over his perfect lips. "You occupy 96.2548 percent of my brain activity. I had the only Mensa friend who will still talk to me measure it yesterday. He said I'm totally fucked, and I should just roll over and let you consume the other 3.7452 percent and call it a day." He chuckles and stares deep into my eyes while I get lost in the delicate pattern of his irises. Jesus Christ, even the pattern in his irises turn me on.

"Did you plan that statement or rattle those numbers off from the top of your head?" I ask, as my smile widens and his eyes sparkle in the light of the late afternoon sun beaming in from the nearby window.

"I'm a math whiz. There. I said it. Now forget about my mad math skills and let me take you to my pleasure dome." His eyebrows wriggle at me, and I cannot help but bust out in a full belly laugh. That was so sexy. Max makes me laugh, always seems to have everything under control, and I'm in awe of him.

Max holds my chin in his grasp, takes my mouth, and kisses me so deeply that I'm tingling with excitement. He gazes longingly at me, his expression screaming passion, then he holds my hand and leads me to his bedroom. I stand at the edge of his bed while he rips off his white t-shirt. He stares at me again with a look of shameless desire, then presses me down gently to the bed and crawls over my body.

"Is this what you had in mind when you drove that sweet ass car of yours here tonight?"

"Yes."

"That's perfect. You're going to do everything I say. Is that alright?" he asks, his tone deep and powerful.

"Yes, please," I answer without hesitation.

A wry smile eases over his perfect lips, and I smile back. Max takes the lead in removing each piece of my clothing in a slow sensual manner that has me internally screaming for him to move faster. He smiles wider as more and more of my body gets exposed to him. While he pulls my bra away from my shoulders, he kisses a trail along my torso, stopping just an inch away from my mound. I hitch a breath when he nears my sex with his mouth as I'm dying for him to do for me what he did in the loft.

"Am I allowed to talk?" I ask to clarify what the game rules are.

"You can talk all you want, but you cannot tell me what to do. I'd rather hear you moan when I make you feel good." Another trip down my torso with his tongue tasting my skin send goosebumps racing down my arms. I reach out to run my fingers through his hair, wanting desperately to press his mouth south to my aching clit, but I think that gesture would also be breaking the game's rules.

"Your skin is so silky. I'm going to tease every inch of your body until you are dripping wet for me and dying for my cock to sink inside of you." I tug at his hair in my fingers, and this makes him chuckle. "You can't have me until I want you to have me, Olivia. Don't be so impatient."

I can't help but moan as my hips writhe beneath him in building anticipation that will surely drive me mad before he gives me what I want. I press my hips up to grind myself against his swollen cock hiding inside his jeans. I may not be able to tell him what to do with my words, but I can act out my desires with my body. Am I bending the rules? Hell, yes.

When Max brings his face back up to mine, I lean forward to kiss him. He accepts me, and I'm not disappointed in how his tongue dances with mine. I don't know where he learned to kiss like this, but it is divine. When his lips break away from me, I begin to pant. My clit is thumping so much harder now.

Max takes that amazing mouth of his and sucks on each of my

nipples just long enough to make them pucker to hard pink nibs and send shivers down my spine. "That's what I want to see," he says. "These nipples have been begging me to tease them." Another longer, harder suck on each of them brings a heightened level of pleasure to me. A small tug with his teeth, another long suck, and then a breath of cool air as he blows over them makes them harder than they've ever been. My hands grip the sheets at either side of me, as I press my shoulders back to arch my chest toward him while I silently beg for more bites, licks, and teasing of my nipples.

Max takes my mouth for a quick kiss then sucks at the side of my neck just below my earlobe. An erogenous zone I had no idea existed has been found. I must learn to regulate my breathing as I'm becoming parched. My mouth is dry, yet my sex is soaking wet. While he continues to explore my neck with his mouth, his thumb graces my clit with a slow circular tease. Then he smooths his thumb down the length of my sex and slips it inside of me.

At last, he's addressing my most urgent need. Deep inside of me, pressing in and out in a slow tease, my entire body relaxes as he asks me, "You like that, don't you?" I nod and lick my lips, and with closed eyes, I focus on the sensation.

"Spread your legs for me." He pulls his thumb out to stroke my sex with my wetness, circling my clit once again. It is so sensitive now from the long wait to be addressed that I can feel myself teetering on the edge with each circle and stroke.

I feel two fingers plunge deep inside while his thumb continues to rub around my clit. I don't know what to focus on when so much pleasure is being applied in unison. "You're so close. I can feel it, Olivia. Are you ready to come for me?"

I nod vigorously as my hands clench at the sheets again. "So close. Don't stop," I murmur.

He chuckles at me. "You cannot tell me what to do, Olivia.

That would be breaking the rules." He stops his teasing as a punishment for my request, and a hint of anger rushes through my head. I'm so desperate to come, and he had me there. He knew I was there, so close, so ready to give in and have the best orgasm I'll have in my life. I realize I'm angrier with myself for speaking as I was doing so well with halting my commands. *Play the game right, Olivia, I remind myself. Do what he asks and you'll get what you need.*

My punishment is short-lived, and I can breathe a sigh of relief. His routine of plunging and circling begins again slowly. I want him to pound his fingers fast and hard inside me like a good old-fashioned finger fuck, but I don't dare demand he do anything. It will be his clit stimulation that is going to take me over the edge. I focus on the movements of his thumb, but then that suddenly stops too. What in the hell is he doing to me? I want to grab a fistful of his hair and pull his face up to mine and let me stare into his soul to scold him silently. But then he'd kiss me again, and I'd melt like a pat of butter in the hot sun.

He holds all the cards. I'm not used to being given so much pleasure in such a long tease, and I'm forming a love-hate relationship with it. My reward for being a good player in the game comes when his mouth and tongue find my clit and begin to lick and suck.

"That's it. There it is," I say through my panting breaths. Oh, my god, oh – my - god," I say, my voice escalating just seconds before I release. My eyes have rolled back inside my head, my shoulders tense, and my hands grapple blindly for any part of Max that I can touch.

His tongue laps at my sex as I'm wrung out with my release. "Holy fuck," I say as I shudder while the remnants of my orgasm escape me. Max kneels on the bed between my legs and begins to undo his belt. A well-deserved satisfied grin beams down at my exhausted, sweat coated body, and I have to wonder what he has in store for me next.

97

The Art of Love in New York City

The belt slips loose from the loops of his jeans as his eyes flash at me. "I want to tie your hands up over your head with my belt, Olivia."

I nod and lick my parched lips again. His smile widens like he's just won the lotto, and I giggle. I need him inside me, and I cannot wait to watch him undo those jeans to reveal that beautiful cock to me. I get what I wish for as he removes his jeans and black boxers before climbing back over me to tie my hands with his belt. His hard as steel shaft lays tantalizingly close to my face as he cinches the belt around my wrists over my head. I chance an opportunity to wrap my mouth around him, and he chuckles at me.

"Do you want a taste? I might let you have a taste, but you aren't allowed to make me come like this," he commands. My hands are now secure above my head. He eases his shaft closer to my mouth, and I open wide to receive him. I get a sweet little taste of his pre-cum on my lips, and I let my tongue circle his crown before he dips inside my mouth a little deeper.

I suck gently when he pulls away from my lips, and then he slips inside my throat a bit deeper this time. He groans at my teasing and tasting of him. Max goes in for a third press inside my mouth then pulls away completely.

"I need you inside of me, Max," I say. "I'm not telling you what to do; I'm just begging you to let me feel you fill me." A tender, sweet, wet kiss graces my lips as the euphoria of the moment gets deeper.

He enters me with a full deep plunge, and I'm in heaven. Each press is with purpose and need. His lips pull at my nipples again while he presses methodically in and out of me. I watch his face as he indulges in his building orgasm. My hips meet his as he pumps harder and faster. "Come for me," I whisper. His mouth finds mine willing to indulge in a hard kiss that finishes with a bite of my lower lip. And just then, the last of his quickened deep thrusts culminates in his blissful release.

Max takes a few slow breaths before he collapses atop me, sated and happy. I am just as happy. Never happier. He kisses me sweetly before removing the belt from my wrists. I cannot wipe the smile off my face. Nobody has ever ventured to tie my hands, and it felt good to submit to him, his desires, and to play the game within the rules he made. I've never wanted any man the way I want, Max.

Chapter 18 – Max

I'm not sure where Olivia's mind is as we rest together in this hug, savoring this moment while the euphoria of what we shared slowly fades. My desires for her will not fade. Every time I'm with her, near her, I feel things I've not felt before. "Where did you go?" I ask, wondering what is on her mind since she is so quiet.

"Nowhere. I'm here," she says while her face is tucked beneath my chin and her soft breaths warm my skin.

"What are you thinking about?"

"If I tell you, I might scare you off," she says, sounding worried. She lifts her head to look at me.

I chuckle and kiss her cheek. "I highly doubt that. Try me?"

Her face curls a little to the left to face me full on. Her eyes meet mine, and I cannot help but smile.

"How did we get to this place, this specific place where a few phone calls and two lunch dates culminated in such a torrid affair? I mean, don't get me wrong, but why is the only question on my mind, where have you been all my life?" Her eyes continue to search mine while she says what is in her heart. My only reaction is to nod in acceptance of her concern.

"We're both asking ourselves the same question, Olivia. But does it feel wrong to you?"

"No. God, no. That isn't what I was saying," she replies quickly. Olivia rolls over to her side before climbing over the top of my body. Does it feel wrong to you?" she asks, throwing my question back to me.

"Not on your life. I refuse to think this is wrong on any level. We're adults who happened to find each other when we needed to." I place my hands on her hips and stroke her skins with my palms. "The length of time it takes for two people to connect either physically or emotionally is not relevant. I'd never considered that I'd be a 'love at first sight' kind of guy, but few things surprise me anymore."

She nods and kisses me. It is a long, smolderingly, passionate kiss that is making me so fucking hard for her again. While the intensity of our kiss grows, I feel a tear from her eye land upon my cheek, shocking me out of our momentary bliss. "Are you crying? Please don't cry. God, what did I do to make you cry?"

Olivia smiles and laughs at herself. "I'm just so happy now, and I guess this is a little overwhelming to me. I'm an emotional mess."

I wipe the tear on her cheek while she continues to express herself.

"Between what's happening with Carl; divorcing a man I thought I'd live the rest of my life with, finding a new place to live, and having the best sex ever with a guy I've grown crazy for and known for less than a few weeks, it hit me like a wave and I lost myself. But these are happy tears, Max. Don't think for a minute otherwise."

"Okay, Olivia. And ditto on the best sex of my life comment. You, my gorgeous girl, literally have me by the heart and balls." I wriggle my eyebrows at her, and she laughs at me.

"Oooh. Whatever will I do with all this power over you?" She wipes her hand across her cheek once more and then playfully taps at the edge of her chin, pretending to be pondering her options. I flip her over on the bed to her back and stare down at her, nose to nose.

"That kind of power is dangerous," I say. "Be careful how you wield it."

She continues to search my soul with those amazing eyes of hers as a slow grin forms over her lips. I try to stay expressionless, but I can't. "I'm totally fucked, aren't I?" I ask. She nods, and we both break out into full belly laughs. I am most definitely fucked.

We cuddle and laugh at each other for a while longer. My stomach growls as her head lays upon my abdomen. "We forgot to eat."

"I'm hungry now too. Give me five in the bathroom, and I'll meet you in the kitchen."

We sit down at the dining room table to eat the dinner I'd prepared in advance. The pasta was a little dry, having been sitting in the oven on warm for nearly an hour, but Olivia didn't complain one bit. Halfway through our meal, she wants me to explain who Kelsey is to me, and a lump forms in my throat at the thought of having to discuss that woman with anyone.

I swallow hard and clear my throat. "I don't like to grace her with the dignity of mentioning her name to anyone, but since you've had the displeasure of meeting her and seeing the ugly side of me when she's in my presence, I guess I owe you the full story."

I lean back in my chair and toss my napkin over my plate. "When I opened up my agency six years ago, Kelsey was the first realty agent I hired. My brother and I were excited to have an established agent with an excellent reputation on our team.

As a businesswoman, Kelsey knocks it out of the park. I mean, she really knows her stuff, how to engage with people and how to close a deal like few others I've known in this business. Within a few months of her working for us, she and I started seeing each other."

"I got that impression from her in our brief encounter. She

oozed confidence," Olivia says as she holds her chin in her palm with her elbow resting on the table.

I take a big gulp of my wine and continue my story. "Anyway, we became close over the next year, and as much as I cared for her, I never felt true love for her. We were good together due to common interests, connections with friends, the sex was good and regular, she was attractive and looked after herself, but I didn't fall in love with her. One day she asked me if I were interested in marriage, and I told her I wasn't ready to marry her. A month later, she informs me that she is pregnant, so I did what most guys in that situation would do; I analyzed our overall relationship and thought that I might not love Kelsey, but everything else about her is perfect. More than anyone could really ask for."

Olivia nods at me and seems quite interested to see where this story is going. She refills her wine glass and says, "Carry on." I take in a deep breath and do as Olivia asks.

"A week later I bought her a ring, proposed to her in the most romantic place I could think of, and she accepted. We were engaged. I realized that it wasn't such a bad idea, after all. Once I'd done the deed, I was over my concerns about being madly in love with a woman before I'd marry them. We had a kid on the way, and I was sure she'd make a great mom, and I was growing excited about the prospect of being a dad. Two out of three ain't bad, right?"

Olivia nods, and a small smile comes my way. "You are a very honorable guy, Max. Not all men would stick around and take that kind of responsibility seriously."

I smile at Olivia's support of my decision, but I'm not sure she's going to like how I handled part two of the story. I start fidgeting with my fork while I continue. "So, nearly four months go by, and I'm in full daddy mode now.

The Art of Love in New York City

I started squirreling away as much money as I could from the moment she told me we were having a baby, knowing kids aren't cheap. I got a great deal on a minivan and parked it at my parent's place until Kelsey and I could decide where to buy a house in the burbs after our child was born. I was secretly reading books on raising kids and how to be supportive of the new mom. I even took cooking classes once a week while Kelsey did her Pilates classes so I could make my new family decent meals when she was sick or otherwise occupied.

I became immersed in the concept of raising a family, maybe two or three kids, envisioning a white picket fenced yard, a dog or two, parties in the back yard with our new neighbors, all that shit. I pause to refill my wine glass and take another sip, then blow out a long breath as I set the glass down on the table.

"In those first few months of our engagement, she tried desperately to get me to go to City Hall and have a quickie marriage and plan a proper full wedding after the baby was born. I hummed and hawed over that. I wanted to wait until the baby arrived and do a big wedding with friends and family. The City Hall thing didn't sit right in my head. As those months passed, I noticed Kelsey was hiding her naked body from me more and more. I thought she was worried that I'd not find her attractive as her belly grew, but that wasn't the case at all. The truth was she wasn't pregnant. I only found out after overhearing a conversation with her and her best friend over the phone. I swear I blew a blood vessel in my neck when I realized I'd been had by her lies. I don't take that kind of betrayal lightly, and I fucking lost it on her."

Olivia's eyes bug out at the truths I'm relaying to her. This is not a new story for a lot of people. Maury Povich made an entire second act career out of outing people who have lied or cheated on their significant others, and I was merely one more of those victims. I shake my head as I recall how fucking mad I was at her. I take a deep breath, finish the wine in my glass before I finish my story to a very wide-eyed Olivia.

"I fired Kelsey immediately, threw her sorry ass out of my apartment, sold the minivan for a loss to get the fucking thing out of my life, and burned all the baby books in my dad's back yard firepit while getting blackout drunk with my brother. It was not a good scene, and I was a mess for many months later. I even rejected any deal or offer that came to my office, which was connected to Kelsey just to make her life as miserable as possible. It took me a long time to trust anyone," I admit, a bit ashamed at how poorly I handled myself afterward.

Olivia's eyes are soft on me as she reaches her hand across the table to touch me. "Now I understand why you hate her so much. I assumed the problem with her was related to her cheating on you or something, or making you lose a crapload of money on a deal somehow, but what she did was much worse. I'm not a fan of the way you talk to her in public, but I understand where that anger comes from now. I've also learned that you are passionate about trust, as am I."

"Come here," I say as I pull her arm and need her to sit on my lap. She obliges, and we kiss and hold each other like the bruised souls we are.

"Can I spend the night here with you?"

"Yes, of course. Whatever you want, Olivia. I'm yours, however you need me."

Chapter 19 – Olivia

I wasn't expecting Carl's lawyer's divorce documents to be prepared so quickly, but as I hold them in my hands, my emotions get the best of me. I came to sit in my studio to relax, clear my head and begin a new watercolour painting based on how much I've fallen for Max these past weeks as my inspiration to create an abstract vision of love. We gel together so well. It's like he and I have known each other all our lives. I never felt like this with Carl. For us, it was a constant learning process. He was set firmly in his ways, and I often attributed this to him being ten years my senior. But in truth, the age difference was never the problem. I forgave him all his flaws, as I assumed he forgave mine. We had our strong social circle, academic interests in common, and he allowed me to breathe in my own space with my art just as I allowed him to hide for hours on end in his den reading books or grading papers from his students. It was a simple, comfortable life.

Not until his stroke and the upending of what we thought was a perfectly fine existence together did I realize how much I was missing. I thought my nature was to please others and not fight the system laid before me, but I was wrong.

There is no turning back now, and even if I could fix what is wrong with my current life, I wouldn't make an effort to do so. I find my pen in my ceramic cup holder on my desk in the studio corner and scribble my name in all the spots flagged by his lawyer on the divorce agreement. Done.

Out with the old and in with the new. I can do this. I'm strong enough to find my own way in the dark. I stuff the signed documents inside the manila envelope and take it downstairs. I place it back on the kitchen table where Carl had left it for me and write the word DONE in bold letters on the front of the envelope. Was that childish to do? Yes. But I don't care anymore. The Carl I married is gone forever. The only connection Carl and I have left is this apartment, and when it's sold, we can go our separate ways without looking back. I text Sasha and Max to tell them I am officially a free woman as of today.

Sasha feels bad for me and offers to buy me lunch, and Max is excited for me and wants to take me on a trip to Los Angeles to meet his brother and celebrate my new single status. I decide to take them both up on their respective offers. I'll have lunch this afternoon with Sasha, then fly out to LA tomorrow with Max for a little getaway.

Sasha is a bit of a mother hen to me. She wasn't always this way, but when her only child, a beautiful daughter named Mikka, died suddenly in a car accident, my relationship with Sasha became more protective in nature. I wonder if our sister-like connection, especially after the accident, made Sasha feel the need to find someone else to protect. Healing from a sudden loss, particularly a child, can manifest in many different ways. I, too, mourned Mikka's passing as if she were my own because Carl and I didn't have children, and of course, because her mother is my dearest friend. I adore Sasha and all her devotion to me but smothering me at this time isn't what I need.

Once we are seated in the restaurant, I offer my thoughts. "Sasha. I know you worry, but please don't coddle me. I'm happy to be free again, and I want you to be happy for me too. I've got a good friend and lover in Max, my art is becoming more visible in the marketplace, thanks mostly to you of course, and I just want to spread my wings and let the wind carry me for a while. Do you understand what I'm saying?" I ask as I hold both of her hands clasped in mine at our table in the restaurant.

Sasha smiles at me and blows me an air kiss. "I do. Maybe I'm a bit jealous of you, and I'm subconsciously trying to hold you down because of it. I'm sorry, my love. You know I would do anything for you, just as you would do anything for me. I don't want to hold you back from what you need to do, but I worry that you and Max are moving too fast. Slow down a bit, will you?" she urges as she squeezes my hands in hers. I nod and air kiss her back.

"Yes, Sasha. I will be mindful of my actions and take things slower with Max."

After my luncheon with Sasha, I head back to my apartment to pack my suitcase. Max and I will be away for five days, and LA is just as hot as New York is at this time of year; I don't really need to pack many things. Plus, I want to go shopping while I'm down there since I've not updated my wardrobe in many months, and I've never shopped for clothes in LA.

When we arrive at the LA airport, Russell is there in his car to pick us up. He whisks us to our hotel straight away, and then we will join him later that evening for dinner in the hotel restaurant.

I find Russell to be entertaining. He has as great a sense of humor as Max does, and his wife, Nadine, seems to be a real sweetheart. She promised to take me shopping to her favourite places tomorrow while Max and Russell talk business at the LA office.

Overall our five-day mini-break was wonderful. We dined out every night, sometimes alone and other times with friends or associates of Max's. We cuddled and made love in the hotel room each night and drank entirely too many bottles of wine. The trip felt more like a honeymoon than it did a mini-vacation with my lover.

On the following Friday, Max will attend an awards ceremony, and he's asked me to join him as his plus one. This is a yearly event for real estate agents in the State of New York. Independent agencies and larger corporate agencies receive awards for agents with the highest sales, and other coveted recognitions. It's a formal ceremony, so I'm wearing a classic little black dress and a string of pearls while Max dons a smashingly handsome dark teal silk suit with a white shirt and a burgundy tie. Damn he looks fine in a suit. I feel like a movie star with my arm linked in his as we arrive at the venue and get seated near the front at one of the large round tables in The Empire State Ballroom of the Wyatt New York hotel and convention center.

When we are seated at our table, Max does a little walk around the three tables next to ours, noting the names of the agents who have been assigned seats. I don't know what he's looking for, but I let him wander the tables before he heads to the bar to get us drinks. I'm a bit anxious about meeting his associates, but I'm sure I'll feel more comfortable once the event begins. When Max returns to our table with our cocktails, he looks a bit put off.

"What's the matter, Max?"

"Nothing, Olivia. I noticed as I walked around the tables that Kelsey is sitting just over there behind us, and I had hoped her table would be further away from ours." Max takes a long sip of his Bourbon then smiles at me. "It will be fine. Our backs are facing her table, so unless she wins an award tonight, we don't have to see her smug face," he says, chuckling.

I smile and nod. I take a sip of my wine and comment on how nice the flavor is, then reach for his hand under the table and squeeze it. "Are you or anyone in your agency up for an award tonight?"

"Our sales numbers were outstanding this year, but I'm not certain we've matched that of our stiffest competitor. They win the highest sales rank award nearly every year, but I think we may have given them a run for their money this time. Fingers crossed that we crush them," he says as he takes another long sip of his drink, then kisses me deeply as if nobody can see us. I flush with a hint of embarrassment when one of his colleagues taps Max on the shoulder and tells us to "save it for later." I run my fingers over my lips and wonder if my lipstick is smeared while Max comments back to his colleague, "Don't stare, get your own," then cracks up as he inspects my lips to assure me I'm fine. I pop my makeup mirror out of my purse to double-check because I don't believe him and am relieved that my lipstick is still intact.

As with most ceremonies, there is a lot of chit-chat at the beginning explaining how the awards program works, what the entertainment and meals being served this evening are, and what the current state of the real estate market is expected to be like in the coming year. It is nearly an hour before there is a break in the presenting speakers, and our dinners are served. There must be two-thousand people here tonight. I'm a bit overwhelmed by the size of this event. Max tells me there are roughly twenty-seven thousand active real estate agents in Manhattan alone, and this event is open to the top one percent of the active agents operating in New York City. He also told me that the event is live online for those interested in watching or who could not attend. Suddenly I feel overly conscious of my appearance and hope that my face is not being televised over the internet. I'm not one for wanting to be in the limelight, but Max doesn't seem to mind.

I'm feeling more anxious than I should. I sip my wine as I scan the surrounding tables then Kelsey's face comes into view. Our eyes lock and she smiles and waves at me. God. What do I do now?

Chapter 20 – Max

I remind myself to slow down on the bourbon as the server refills our water glasses. The award for the top-selling agent is saved for the later part of the evening, and the last thing I need is to be drunk if my name is called.

Olivia has been quiet for most of the night. She seems a bit nervous, and I have to remind her from time to time to relax. She nods at me like she heard what I said, but that doesn't stop her from fidgeting with her hands and getting up repeatedly to use the ladies' room. I fully expected that she would be vibrant and lively with conversation with the other people at our table tonight. I'll have to ask her tomorrow why she was apprehensive about filtering her way into the conversations more readily.

Once again, she taps me on the leg under the table to get my attention to say she's going to the ladies' room. When she stands to leave the table this time, she stumbles a bit in her high heels, and I wonder if she's had a bit too much wine. We've been here for nearly two hours, and I've not noticed her drinking any water. I frown at her and ask her if there is something wrong with her bladder. "No. I just want to stretch my legs a bit and take a breather."

"Are you okay? Have you had a bit too much wine?"

"No. I'm fine. I'll drink water when I come back to the table."

"Okay. Don't be too long."

One of the agents at our table is becoming a nuisance now that he's on his tenth beer. He's a great guy when sober but is an obnoxious drunk. I politely exit the table to use the men's room and see if I can locate Olivia in her walkabout to stretch her legs. I also wouldn't mind stepping outside to smoke a cigar, and maybe she will

The Art of Love in New York City
join me.

As I weave my way between the chairs from table to table to reach the convention room's perimeter pathway, I'm stopped by a few familiar faces who want to say hello and chat briefly. They all wish me good luck at winning the top sales award since everyone knows I'm one of three names on the award ballot from the schedule of events booklet provided for each table. I nod, shake hands, and laugh at their jokes.

When I'm finally free of the puzzle path to the walkway, I straighten my jacket and head toward the washrooms in the outside corridor. I step outside of the convention room doors and realize I've spilled something from dinner on my suit, which pisses me off.

How did that happen? I was so careful not to spill on my suit while I was eating. "Shit," I mutter to myself as two women pass me to enter the convention room. They smile as I reach to hold the door for them, and then I continue on my way to head to the washrooms near the end of the carpeted corridor.

Upon approaching the ladies' room entrance, I hear the voices of two women talking, and then they are suddenly silent. Naturally, I turn my head to look at who the women are and assume they stopped talking as they heard me near them.

My heart arrests in my chest when the sight of Olivia being kissed passionately by Kelsey fills my eyes. "What in the fucking hell is this bullshit?" I rage as I grab Olivia by her arm and spin her around to face me. She is startled by my presence and stumbles a bit in her heels once she's been turned around before me. Her eyes widen as she registers it's me demanding to know what she's doing making out with Kelsey behind my back. Olivia stammers to speak to me, then Kelsey overpowers Olivia's words with her wicked tongue.

"You have excellent taste in women, Max. Who knew your Olivia was such a wonderful kisser and a complete knockout in the looks department? Did you know she swung both ways?"

I've seen the colour red in my eyes before amid Kelsey's antics, but nothing could have prepared me for being taken for a fool. I realize my hand still grips Olivia's bicep, and I squeeze it tightly before releasing her with a push back toward Kelsey. "Un-fucking believable," I grind out before storming away to attempt to cool my head. I'm fueled by hatred, rage, and the shock of unfathomable betrayal. Never in my wildest dreams would I have taken Olivia for a bisexual. And least of all, willing to cheat on me with my ex.

The exit door opens automatically in a painfully slow manner as I attempt my swift departure. I stride with purpose down the busy downtown street, bumping the odd passerby's shoulder, heading exactly nowhere in particular. I stop beside the next building, mirrored smoked glass reflecting every move around me. My cigar is somewhere inside this jacket, and I eagerly explore every pocket until I locate it. My hand shakes a little as I snip off the tip and attempt to light it, facing the direction opposing the wind. After several attempts, I get it to spark, and I puff hurriedly on the Cuban classic to ensure that it's lit. The first full puff of smoke escapes my lungs slowly, seeping from my mouth like silky dry ice floating across a dance room floor. I catch my reflection in the mirrored wall of the office tower, stare at myself in an attempt to calm the fuck down, but it is proving to be impossible.

I need to think this through. Did I really witness my girlfriend, the woman I can in all honesty say that I'm in love with, kissing my ex-fiancé, my nemesis, in plain sight? Have they been together for a while, or is this something that transpired tonight? Are they drunk and stupid? Is this something Kelsey has been planning behind my back to get back at me? "Jesus fucking Christ!" I yell into the crowded sidewalk, but nobody cares what my problem is.

The shock of Kelsey's unexpected kiss, the disbelief that Max witnessed it, and his reaction rage through me like a tidal wave. My eyes wide, my heart pounding, and my anger rising, I'm prompted to shove Kelsey up against the wall and stare her down. "What the fuck was that about?"

Kelsey laughs and attempts to kiss me again. I want to slap her across the face, but my palms fist at my sides, knowing the least lady-like thing to do at a function like this is to make a public scene. Two women pass us in the entry separating Kelsey and me from our close contact. "You are a spiteful, manipulative bitch," I grind out in the lowest voice I can muster.

More laughter comes at me as she presses past my body to leave the restroom. I have a mind to take my purse and slam it against the back of her head, but I need to find Max and explain what he witnessed. He has to know this was a setup, and we are both victims of Kelsey's bullshit attempts to make Max jealous.

I cannot imagine Max would head back inside the ballroom after seeing him so fired up with anger. He must have gone outside, but which door did he use to exit? My eyes search back and forth down the corridor for exit doors, and I note two of them are near the restrooms. I chance that it is the one on the left and head outside the hotel to scan the street. It is difficult to pick out a familiar face in the crowd of pedestrians even with stilettos on, giving me a higher vantage point. If he went through this exit, would he have gone left or right? I growl to myself in frustration knowing that no matter which way I decide to walk in search of Max, I may never find him.

It's been nearly ten minutes since the incident with Kelsey, and Max could have gone anywhere. I resign to head back inside the ballroom to my seat at the table. I can only hope that he has returned or will soon. I'm sure of one thing; he will not want to miss his award presentation should he be the top producer this year. With fingers crossed, I make a swift reappearance to our table, but Max is nowhere in sight.

The other realtors at our table smile and nod at me when I sit down, and I try to look unscathed by recent events. I don't dare turn my back to look for Kelsey as I wouldn't want her to have the pleasure of my eyes on her. Knowing her, she'd take that as an invitation and I cannot risk her thinking I am interested in her on any level.

I become more nervous as I wait for Max to return. Did he leave without me, forgoing the chance to stand before his peers with a well-deserved award? My head continues to twist left to right glancing over the tables and the entry doors to the ballroom intermittently in hopes he has decided to come back. I cannot take not knowing where he is and decide to call his cell. As expected, I get his voicemail, but I must leave him an impassioned plea to make him understand that I wasn't receptive to Kelsey's actions.

"Max. That wasn't what it looked like. Please come back to the ballroom and let me explain." Nearly forty minutes have passed since the incident at the restrooms, and I can't stand to stay here alone any longer, fielding questions of Max's whereabouts to the other table guests. Without a word of interruption to the other members of our table, I rise, grab my sweater and purse and leave the ballroom without attracting anyone's attention.

When I enter the corridor that leads to the reception area of the hotel, I make one more attempt to call Max. Again I am ignored by him, and the call goes to voicemail. "Max, I'm going home. I cannot sit at this table without you. Please, I'm begging you to call me back the minute you get my messages."

The hotel valet secures a cab for me at my request. I'm trying desperately not to lose my composure during the drive home, but a tear escapes my eye regardless. When I arrive home, I am emotionally exhausted, still a little drunk, and cannot wait to rest my body upon my bed. With my cell phone placed on the side table, I kick off my shoes and climb inside my bed with my clothes on. I don't want to cry anymore, but the emotions flow in streams down my cheeks again. I must have cried myself to sleep as I didn't hear the text tone sound out when Max replied to me at one in the morning.

When I rose from my pillow, the smudges of mascara are a reminder of how tragic last night was to my heart. I pick my cell phone up off the side table and see the text Max sent while I slept. "There is no forgiving what you did to me."

"No, Max," I say exasperatedly to my empty room. My fingers fly across the cell phone screen, typing a reply message that I can only hope he will take seriously. "How could you think that I would betray you? Where is this coming from? You need to talk to me, Max."

Chapter 22 – Max

I awaken determined not to let Olivia or Kelsey destroy me. I'll do what I always do when my personal life goes into a tailspin; I focus on my work. I had won the top sales agent award for the previous year's sales record, but somehow, that win feels hollow. I should be proud of myself and my team for their work to help me achieve such a coveted award to display in my office. My immediate plan is to gather all my agents and reward them with lunch and the bonus checks I promised if we won. We are a team, and as much as I love having my name on the trophy, this award belongs to us all.

I have blocked any future calls or texts that come from Olivia. She promised me heaven while leading me down a road to hell—a hell I'd already visited once before with the same devil in the driver's seat. I have forgiven few in my lifetime, and for good reason. My heart and my head have betrayed me, and it appears I am back at square one in the search for a woman who doesn't have an agenda that involves hurting me. Or is it that I'm simply not cut out to be the marrying kind? Yet, as much as I am destroyed by her actions, a little piece of me wants to believe I've been had only by Kelsey. I've never felt so much love for another person before Olivia, and her messages seemed impassioned.

I chalk up my small bit of doubt as to her intentional betrayal of me to that intense love during our short-lived affair. My gut tells me this is another attempt by Kelsey to attack me where I'm most vulnerable. Would she stoop that low, to take my lover from me for spite? How long is Kelsey going to hold her grudge against me? And who am I really punishing here? Myself or Olivia? My natural reaction is to punish Kelsey, but what if Olivia isn't innocent?

The devil on my shoulder wants to believe the worst while the angel on the other shoulder begs me to look deeper into the situation and let Olivia give me her side of the story. I need more time before I can let her speak her mind. My phone is ringing off the hook from my peers congratulating me on the sales award and realtors looking to join my team. The sharks circle looking for a piece of my temporary celebrity status in the real estate world of New York City.

I should feel like a king, walking around with my chest puffed out and standing outside my shop, proud and filled with wide-eyed anticipation like the Pilgrims landing on Plymouth Rock must have felt. I have a new frontier. I've outsold my competition for the first time since my brother and I began this journey six years before. I realize that I need to sit down and lay out my goals for the coming year. During my lunch with my team, I'll fill them in on my expectations and work together to ensure we are in the running to win the top sales award again next year.

My phone rings and vibrates across the top of my desk. I flip it over and see it is Russell calling me to congratulate us on winning the top sales award. "Hello, Russell," I say smugly into my phone.

"Hello, Max. Nice work on the award, bro. Where are you going to display that fancy trophy?"

"Right where everyone can see it the minute they walk into the office. The glass case behind reception, I think," I say as I reach for my coffee cup. "What's new in LA?"

"Business is still doing well. I've hired two new agents who will start this week, both of which I think you'll like. They are a team of their own, and I scooped them away from the Garrison Agency a few days back."

"Nice. And are we still on target for sales? What is the comparable from last month?" I ask. I see my receptionist hovering by my office door, and I raise my coffee mug to her to let her know I need a refill. She comes in all smiles and retrieves my mug.

"So I saw on the live feed that you took Olivia with you. But she didn't stick around to see you accept your award. What the fuck was that about?" he asks.

I palm my forehead, then pinch the bridge of my nose. "Jesus. It is too long of a story to tell you right now. We're done. That's all I can say. Let me explain that one to you later."

"It seems to me, Max, that you have been playing the field a little too long. When the fuck are you going to settle down? I mean, I'm four years younger than you, married and planning a family, and you're still trying to find a woman who will date you more than once. Time to get your shit together, don't you think?" Russell chuckles at me, and I chuckle back at him.

"I haven't found the right girl. You got lucky." I lean back in my chair and throw my feet up atop my desk. My receptionist returns to me with a fresh cup of coffee, setting it down on my desk next to my feet. I thank her quietly while Russell continues to rib me about my dating issues. "Listen, smart ass. I don't need my baby brother giving me advice on dating women. I taught you the ropes, remember?"

"All I want to say, and don't take this the wrong way, Max, but I'm beginning to wonder if it is you that is the problem and not the women you are dating. There is an art to love, Max. Think about that for a minute. Nobody seems good enough for you. What are you looking for? And has every woman you ever dated really at fault for the ending of your relationships? Take a page from your own advice book, bro; the bigger treasure is below the surface. Dig deeper."

"Oh, so now you're throwing my advice back at me. Fine. Thanks for the Ted talk. Same time next week?"

"Later, Max," he says and then hangs up on me. I shake my

head and take my feet off my desk. Maybe he's right, but I'd never admit that to Russell, or I'd never hear the end of it. I take a sip from my coffee and go back to my paperwork since romance seems to be the one thing I have no control over.

While I'm jotting down notes for my luncheon speech, my secretary pops inside my office with a package. Before I begin to open it, she tells me she'll draw the office blinds so the staff can see what an award-winning real boss looks like when he's working. I chuckle at her and tell her to get back to her desk. "What a real boss looks like working," I say, repeating her cheeky words while I unwrap the package. I'm so involved in untying the elaborate wrapping that I don't notice my staff and sales team gathering around the glass walls that separate my office from the bullpen.

The box feels light as I cut the last string with the scissors and pry it open with the tips of my fingers. A blast of confetti, spiral strings, and sparkles explodes in the air around me. "Russell! I'm going to kill that bastard," I yell.

He sent me a glitter bomb. I'm now fully aware of the crowd outside my walls who are in hysterics as I stand amid the biggest mess I've ever seen. I cannot help but laugh and wave at my audience. They all try to squeeze inside my office to talk about the mess and laugh at me being had by my stupid brother. I immediately dial Russell's cell phone to give him shit. I put the call on speaker for everyone to hear, and when he answers, the first words out of my mouth are, "Russell, you fucker!" His laughter fills the space.

"Please tell me somebody got that on video!" he replies. A few voices pipe up with a resounding yes. "Good to know. Send it to me!"

I shoo everyone out of my office so Russell and I can continue our conversation. A similar awards program exists for L.A., but I don't think my satellite office will be near the ranks of the big boys down there. It will be a few more years of clawing our way into the wallets of the whales before we see awards for sales records in L.A.

"You are *such* an asshole, Russell. Do you have any idea how much of a mess these things are?" I'm trying to be mad, but he got me good. "I'll send your office the bill for the clean-up."

He chuckles at me. "Sure, Max."

"And remember that no good deed goes unpunished, asshole."

Chapter 23 – Olivia

As I lay upon my bed, I yearn for Max's touch again. My eyes close as the sun sets in the background, slowly darkening my quiet space.

In my mind's eye, I see his masculine form standing beside me at the edge of my bed. My sex begins to ache as I watch him remove his shirt and look upon me with warmth in his eyes.

He doesn't need to speak or ask me anything to understand what I need from him. The sensation that I can't control increases between my legs as I imagine his cock growing aroused, and this ache I feel between my legs is the equivalent of an erection building that cannot be seen, only felt like pangs of hunger.

His beautiful face hovers briefly over mine before his tender lips touch me. My desire builds in intensity, and I want his hands on me, his lips and fingers playing over my skin, around my sex, testing my resolve to remain still while he explores me.

I continue to envision his warm, broad hand reaching up beneath my blouse to cup my swollen breast. A soft kneading, a small moan from my mouth at the sensuality of his touch, and breaths audible in the room's silence give me comfort. A palm around my face holds me still as he kisses me and whispers his affectionate words in my ear.

The ache of my engorged flesh heads to my clit, and it begins to pulse like the beat of my heart. My nipples immediately respond. I release my bra strap to allow him the access he needs while I imagine his hand, stroking the skin, his open palms circling over my nipples as they pucker with the delight of this playful attention to them. A little tug with his fingers, then his warm lips and tongue bring my need and hunger to the forefront. Bite them, tug them, I beg him in my mind.

While he entertains his desires with his mouth on my full breasts, I feel the heel of his palm slip tantalizingly slow down my belly and press upon my mound. He's near the pulsing flesh, the core of my sexual being, and excitement runs through my spine like the sparks of pain from the small bites he gave my nipples.

He hears me whisper, "*Touch me everywhere. Leave no place bare of your kisses, your hot breaths, your tongue or your hands.*" Two fingers weave between the engorged folds of my throbbing vulva as I hitch a breath knowing the impending sensation is about to prime me for the grand finale.

I grow desperate, hungrier, impatient. The dampness of my arousal makes it easy for his fingers to explore me. They caress, stroke, smooth, and skillfully avoid my clit while I internally scream at him for taking his time. But he wants to enjoy me as much as I need to come. This is what Max does to me. He draws me in, plays with my desires, like a child exploring his options with a new toy. He's curious and in control, and it's so fucking hot.

This massage of my sex calms me like his warm breaths on my cheek. He wants to tell me how hard he is for me in a whisper and trace the tip of his tongue over the edges of my ear.

This tease is only a short distraction from where his fingers are. At last, he finds my clit as swollen as my nipples, throbbing, needing, begging for the long-awaited attention. Max moves slowly, finding the exact spot above my clit to massage then every once in a while, his finger rubs across it, making me gasp with delight. "*Do that again,*" I beg. "*Roll your fingers coated in my arousal over it, repeatedly, a little faster now, don't stop, I'm almost there.*"

My breaths grow heavier and faster, emulating Max's fingers taking my building orgasm to the highest point. At the peak of the intensity, my head thrashes left and right; I let out a small whimper and hold my breath for just an instant when I release.

The Art of Love in New York City

Shoulders relax, my parched lips are moistened by my tongue, another little nip at my ear, and I'm spent. I don't dare open my eyes. He's not here physically, and I know this, but I felt him this entire time like a light breeze that blew through my open window. It caressed my sweat coated skin as gently as his touch. What is this man doing to my mind?

While I drown in my sorrows over Max's refusal to talk to me, I focus on creating another sculpture. My melancholy mood and my choice to play sad, slow songs on my sound system lead me to sketch a dramatic and ambitious project out on paper. I want this sculpture to be big. I want people to walk around it and see something different at every angle, making them question what they think its meaning is. I'm so filled with emotional turmoil now, and I need to channel that into an art piece.

The hours pass while I sketch several different views of the piece as it forms in my visions. All four sides are clear to me now, but since this is a multi-faceted object, I'll need to do a test rendering in modeling clay to get the dimensions right.

Pinning the four view sketches up on my easel, I can see small adjustments that I need to make. I step forward, add more detail, step back, observe, step forward, add more detail, step back. I do this dance for another hour while the sun slowly slinks behind the accumulating clouds taking away my precious studio natural light. Glancing at my watch, I realize that I've not eaten a thing in the past several hours. With luck, Carl is holed up in his den, and I can cook something quick for myself without him in my way.

Our cupboards have been separated into two sides. The cupboards on the left side are the ones I'm using to store my supply of food and spices. Carl's cabinets are on the right. The fridge is set up in the same manner, my stuff on the left, his stuff on the right. This is beginning to look like the War of the Roses. I wouldn't be surprised if Carl starts taping off lines on the floors marking off where I'm allowed to walk and where he's allowed to walk within the apartment.

This thought makes me laugh. I suppose there are worse divorce situations out there in this fine city we call The Big Apple. *"Yeah, take a bite out of this shit,"* I say to myself. I find a can of New England Chowder in my cupboard, which will be a perfect filler until I decide on a small snack later.

Once I've had a bite to eat, I settle down in my bedroom to watch some television. This is not how I envisioned entertaining myself these past few days. I thought I'd be resting my body against Max on his couch, flipping channels on the T.V. until we find something we both want to watch, eating a massive bowl of popcorn and sipping mixed drinks. A lump forms in my throat as the vision I have in my head of who we should be, and what we've become gets the best of me. I promised myself that I'd be better at controlling how I feel. However, Max's refusal to call or text me has burned a hole in my chest that doesn't feel like it will heal anytime soon.

Grabbing my phone off my side table, I send Max one text.

"You can't see the forest for the trees."

I hope he gets the intention of my message. He is so blinded by anger that he's not seeing that I am innocent. I am a victim of Kelsey as much as he is. In fact, from a legal standpoint, Kelsey assaulted me. I neither asked nor tried to lead her on in any manner, which would give her reason to kiss me. One more message to Max, and then I'm done. If this one doesn't make him believe that I'm on his side, nothing will.

"I'm filing charges against Kelsey for assault of my person."

After fifteen minutes, I note that my messages to Max are not going through. That's weird. Has he blocked me? Are you fucking kidding me? Now I'm pissed off. I'm the first to admit when I'm acting childish, but for him to block my calls without giving me at least one chance to defend myself is ridiculous. Tomorrow that boy is getting a piece of my mind, face to face.

Chapter 24 – Max

Busy is as busy does, my mother always said. Funny enough, I can't stop working at full throttle, and that suits me fine. To top off my good mood, I got a text message from Russell to say that a twenty-six-million-dollar home listing we have in Bel Air is sold. I think I'll treat myself to a pricy new suit today with that hefty commission. Armani perhaps. I press my head outside of my office door and yell out to my staff, "The twenty-six-million-dollar listing in L.A. is S – O – L - D!" Cheers and clapping fill the office, and my pride-filled smile isn't going anywhere soon.

I sit back down at my desk to make some important phone calls to clients who are already listed and those still on the fence about pricing for their homes. The real estate market is steady at the moment, and projections indicate it will stay that way for the next six months. I'll use these stats to reassure my hesitant client inquiries to convince them this is a good time to hit the market if they are serious about selling or buying.

I'd just hung up my most recent call when my secretary enters my office to tell me I have a client waiting for me in the reception. My hand immediately rummages through the papers on my desk looking for my appointment book, and I don't see a meeting scheduled for this afternoon written in my calendar. "Did they say they had a meeting and I forgot?"

"No. I think she showed up hoping you were in the office and could talk with her. Do you want me to tell her you're busy?"

"No, don't worry about it. I need a break from my calls anyway. Send her in, please." I straighten out my paperwork mess and make sure there isn't any glitter left on my guest chairs across from my desk. That shit took forever to clean up, and I'm still finding it under my desk, inside my pen holder, and in the folders on my wall shelf behind me. Fucking Russell. I have to find a way to get him back.

I sit myself down in my chair, straighten my tie, and spin around to face the door to my office. I'm about to smile and stand when I see Olivia gracing the entrance to my office. *Shit!*

"Hi, Max," she says, as she proceeds to sit comfortably in the guest chair.

My smile is pensive as I hold back the urge to usher her back out of my office and close the door on her. I only need to see her walking away, not sitting in front of me. I've never felt as betrayed as I did when I saw her kissing with Kelsey. Kelsey, I'd have expected that behavior from, but not my Olivia. It will take me a lifetime to trust another woman again after that incident.

"Max. For the love of God, would you please stop blocking my calls and texts? You haven't even given me two minutes of your time to tell you what happened."

My jaw tightens, and it is everything I have in me not to lose my cool. "I know what I saw, Olivia. I also didn't like what I saw. What is so hard for you to understand? We're over. There is nothing to discuss unless you want to talk about your apartment."

Olivia sighs in exasperation. "Oh, for fuck sakes, Max! Stop being so damned pig-headed."

"You know what? How about you get out of my office and forget that I exist. I don't know what it is that you're looking for, but it isn't here. While I pour myself a shot of Bourbon from the glass cabinet at the side of the desk, I say, "A flaky, lying, bisexual artist like yourself likely has many sources for people to betray with your charms." As I grab the glass, I notice more of that fucking glitter inside the tumbler, which pisses me off more than I already am.

Why does she have to be so attractive to me? Why would she build me up just to tear me down? Who does that? I blow out the inside of the glass with a quick breath, then fill it with roughly two fingers worth of the amber liquid. If I were a gentleman, I'd have offered to pour her a glass to join me, but the asshole in me isn't in the mood to play nice.

Olivia stands as I turn myself around to sit back down in my chair and slaps me across the face. "What the hell is wrong with you?" (she yells).

I touch my chin and scrub my hand across it, then smile. "You excel at the element of surprise, Olivia."

"Well, here's another surprise for you. If you'd read any of my text messages in the last two days, you'd know that I am as much a victim of Kelsey as you are. What the hell, Max! Without warning, Olivia bursts into tears and sits down in the chair behind her. "Why, Max?" she asks between sobs. "Why are you treating me like the enemy?"

I grab two tissues out of the box I hide inside my left drawer and hand them to her. Am I so shrouded with anger from Kelsey that I knee jerk reacted to a loss of trust in Olivia? I worried that because our relationship got hot and heavy so quickly that I was too easily led to the place I'm in now. I pause for a minute and let Olivia calm down. I do owe her the time to explain. Even if I don't like what she has to say, I have to listen at least. My posture relaxes as I down the contents of my cocktail in one gulp. It burns as it goes down, but then, at this moment, my heart is burning in the same way.

"Explain to me what I saw, Olivia," I ask in a calmer tone. I roll my empty tumbler between my palms while I await her answer. I want her to stop crying as everyone in the office can see inside mine. I decide to close my office door for privacy as they are whispering to each other already. Olivia gathers herself as best she can as she scrunches up the damp tissues in her right hand. She dabs her nose with it and clears her throat.

"Kelsey followed me to the restroom and started asking me questions about our relationship. I told her that our connection was through my art; that you bought one of my sculptures, and after two lunches, we started dating seriously. That information seemed to get her back up, and she got a bit indignant with me. Then she started telling me how you dumped her after she lost her pregnancy and threw her out of the house without any explanation."

"She didn't lose the pregnancy. There was no pregnancy," I bite out. My jaw clenches as I remind myself to stay calm. Olivia nods as she dabs her nose once more and asks if she can have a glass of water.

"Yeah, sure. Give me a minute." I pop out of the office and bring her a refrigerated water bottle from the lunchroom. My hand touches hers as she reaches for the water bottle, and my confused heart stills for a moment. She removes the cap from the bottle, takes a long sip and nods.

"I knew your side of the story, and just as I was about to refute her words, she must have spotted you and dove into my face and started kissing me. I had no idea what she was doing until I heard you yell at me. Max, she used me to get to you, and all you saw was exactly what she wanted you to see. Don't you get that?"

I try to keep calm as the image of Kelsey kissing Olivia replays in my head like a bad dream. "How drunk were you?"

"Drunk enough to not understand why you were so mad. But after you grabbed me and yelled in my face, I sobered up instantly. I gave Kelsey a piece of my mind then went searching for you, but you were nowhere to be found."

Olivia takes another long sip of her water and looks down at her lap while she fidgets with replacing the cap on the bottle, then her mood shifts unexpectedly. She takes a deep, shaky breath before continuing. Her eyes narrow as she asks, "Do you really think of me as a flake? That's hurtful, Max. First you don't trust me, and now I'm a flake?" She stands and tries to leave my office while she mutters, "I'm sorry I ever met you. I thought you had so much more respect for me than this. Goodbye."

Her tears fall again as she tries to escape my office. Lunging forward out of my chair, I reach for her arm, but she shrugs me off.

"Enough, Max. You've said how you really feel about me. That's all I needed to know."

"Olivia," (I plead). "Stop for a second, please."

"Why? So you can insult me again? I think I've had enough of that for one day. I may not be as savvy as you in a business sense, but I'm proud of who I am and what I create. I'm not a flake, Max. Go fuck yourself."

I watch in a state of disbelief as she holds her head high and escapes my office. How did this get so turned around on me? I didn't mean what I said. I let my anger get the best of me when I spewed those insults. Fuck! I'm such an idiot. How am I going to make this right?

I escaped to the washrooms down the corridor of Max's office building. If he decides to chase after me, he won't find me here. I need to collect my wits, freshen up my makeup, and stop feeling sorry for myself. I should have known Max and I were too good to be true. No matter how many times Sasha warned me to go easy instead of bolting my way out of the gate like a racehorse, it is clear now the bleeding romantic in me had no control of the reigns. The track was short and the race too fast, but I loved every minute of it. Max made me feel alive again, needed again, hopeful again.

Perhaps this was a simple rebound relationship, and Sasha was right to warn me. But the experiences with both Teddy and Max have meant so much more to me, to my ego, to my personal growth. I've been sheltered in my marriage to Carl. We were solid, unwavering in our nineteen-year monogamous existence. I've never ventured to express my sexuality in other ways until these situations came knocking on my door. Rebound or not, I have grown as a person in recent months.

My cell phone pings with a message, and I'm sure it's Sasha. She knows what I'm going through, and she's worried about my mental state. I want to ignore her and the rest of the world today, but if anyone can put me straight, it's her. I dig my phone out of my purse and read the text.

Max: "I owe you a sincere apology for my actions and my words. Where are you now?"

I stare up at the ceiling and groan. This is what I wanted when I came here today to speak to him. I intended to plead my case and change his mind, but the way he behaved gave me the distinct impression that continuing on is a waste of my time.

He's volatile, has been burned by Kelsey and possibly other women, and now I'm the next in line to question his version of loyalty. Should I ignore his message or text him back? I decide on the latter. This has to end now before we drag ourselves through more anguish. I've already been heartbroken twice in the last month by Carl asking for a divorce, and now I'm going through this trust issue thing with Max. I don't have the strength to fight anymore.

Me: "I accept your apology, but don't come looking for me. We are done, Max."

The following day I find a note on the kitchen table from Carl indicating that he has approved a showing of our apartment by Max at three-thirty this afternoon. I have to chuckle to myself that Carl is now leaving me notes rather than having this conversation face-to-face. Coward.

Throwing the note back on the table, I glance around and decide I need to straighten a few things up before the showing. I begin cleaning the kitchen and bathrooms, even Carl's bathroom since he's nowhere to be found, then a quick dusting and a vacuum seems to make the apartment presentable. My studio is always in a state of flux depending on which art project I'm working on so I'm not going to bother overdoing that space's clean-up.

Now is the time for me to review my financial situation. I've only got eight-thousand dollars left from the sale of Patience to Max. I need this apartment to sell soon so I can move on with my life, but as the days pass, and as the massive rift between Carl and me widens, I'm finding it difficult to feel comfortable in my own home. I should scan the apartment rental listings to look for a small space I can rent for the interim. I need a reboot, a kickstart where nobody can interfere with my vision of my future. No Carl or Max. Just me and my art.

As the time nears for the apartment showing, I realize I need to get myself out of here as I don't want to be near Max. I start to gather my raincoat and umbrella from the downstairs hall closet, preparing to leave, when I hear someone knocking on the door of the upstairs level entry. Janine in apartment 512 likes to invite me over for coffee sometimes, and that's likely her.

I leave my coat and umbrella on the foot of the staircase before running upstairs to open the door. I don't bother looking through the peephole to see who it is as it couldn't be anyone else. The words, "Hi, Janine," come out of my mouth as I open the door, but instead, I see Max standing there. My smile fades in an instant. "You're here too early," I say, as my brow pinches. My tone changes as I speak to him. "And you've come to the wrong door."

"No, Olivia. I'm not at the wrong door," he says as his hands brace either side of the doorway, and his face leans in close to mine.

"Then, what are you doing, Max?" I ask, still being stern.

"This."

Max steps through the doorway, clasps his hands around my face, presses me up against the opposing wall, and drops the most sensual kiss on my lips. Dam him. I cannot help falling for this move while I chide myself for allowing him to take my lips and my heart like this so suddenly. This is unfair – dirty pool. I'm still struggling to get him out of my head and my heart, and now he's decided to forgive all that was wrong in this whirlwind relationship of ours, while I'm trying to stand on my own two feet unencumbered by love, hate, and circumstance.

I allow the kiss to last much longer than I should have. This man fills every void in my life with his passion for me, but I'm not ready for what he has to give. I press his chest with my hands to force him to stop this moment. His lips slowly separate from mine, and his stare holds my heaving chest and confused heart in chains. "Max, we can't do this. I need space, and you need to learn to trust without losing your mind from jumping to conclusions. Neither of those things is going to happen overnight."

I slip past Max to escape his embrace, run my fingers through my hair, and stand tall as he turns to face me in the hallway. "Olivia. You are the one being stubborn now. Can't we go back to where we were? I miss you."

"I'm leaving here soon. I'm renting an apartment for six months, since that is all the money I have left to my name until this apartment is sold. Well, that and the alimony from Carl. I need my space, Max."

I turn to leave to retrieve my raincoat and umbrella from the bottom of the staircase when I hear the lower apartment door open and realize that Carl has returned. Max grabs my arm to halt me.

"Are you sure this is what you want to do? Why don't you stay here and save your money?"

"Money isn't my only issue, Max," I say, releasing myself from his hold on my arm. "Carl's back now. You can discuss the showing with him. I have to leave to look at a rental."

When I descend the stairs, I address Carl. "Max is upstairs waiting for his clients to show up. I'm heading out." I grab my purse and leave from the lower apartment door. Both of those men need to stop messing with my head.

I've found a little one-bedroom apartment in the Bedford-Stuyvesant area of Brooklyn that will temporarily suit my needs. I'm not worried about how posh the address is at this juncture. The area is gritty and bustling with other artists and like-minded people, which should help to keep me inspired and on cue with my immediate goals.

Before I sign the rental agreement for a six-month commitment, I measure the doorway's width and the elevator, so I'm sure any larger sculptures I create while I'm here can safely be transported out of the building. I make a mental note not to make any of my pieces wider than forty-five inches since the narrowest doorway is forty-eight inches.

The unit owner meets me in the building's foyer, standing ready with his contract, and I willingly sign it. Since I agreed to a six-month lease, he gave me a fifty dollar a month discount on the monthly rental cost. My alimony from Carl will cover the rent, and the savings I have will cover the cost of my art supplies and other living expenses. I'll have to be frugal for a while, but I'm up for the challenge.

I return home just past five o'clock to find Carl having a meal of take-out sushi from the restaurant down the block. Once again, I got so busy I forgot to eat. I don't say a word to Carl as I enter the kitchen to find something to make for myself, and he doesn't open his mouth to speak to me either. It's truly pathetic, and for some unknown reason, I break out laughing. Carl turns to see what I'm busting a gut over and frowns at me. "What?" I ask.

"I don't understand you sometimes," he mumbles.

"That is a two-way street, Carl. And for your information, that is precisely what I was laughing about. I know you can't register what our life was like before your stroke, but if you could, you'd be shocked. I never imagined my life changing so dramatically, but here we are—two perfect strangers after nineteen years of marriage. Be honest with me, Carl. It is laughable."

He takes a piece of sushi from his Styrofoam tray and chews slowly. After a moment, he begins to chuckle. I start to laugh again; then, he laughs harder. Now we are both killing ourselves, and neither of us really understands what's going on. This is the best laugh I've had in a long time. My eyes water from the outside corners while Carl's chuckles slowly subside. It dawns on me that this is the first time since his stroke that I've heard him laugh. And it is the first time I've realized that he's happy. We are both happy, regardless of how trying the past year has been.

"What are your plans after the apartment sells?"

"I'm moving to a smaller place closer to the University. It's what I know and where I belong, Olivia. My interest in teaching has never faltered."

I nod as I finish making my sandwich. "I'm going back upstairs. Maybe I'll see you tomorrow sometime," I say as I walk past him sitting at the kitchen table. Carl reaches for my arm as I pass, and I pause.

"You are a good woman, Olivia. Don't think for a minute that I don't appreciate what you've done for me since the stroke. I wish I could be the man I was for you, but I'm not. And I'm sorry if I've hurt you."

A lump forms at the base of my throat. I know now that he is grateful for me, but not in love with me. This I can handle, appreciate, and live with. "Thank you," is all I can say without letting him in on the fact that I'm holding back tears. I move toward the stairs and climb to the top before I let the tears silently fall. The first

The Art of Love in New York City
half of my life's play is over and now begins my intermission.

Chapter 27 – Max

I have always felt that my mission in life was to be successful. I've checked that off my list, and now there seems to be a hollow in my world, and I can only assume it is my need for love. It wasn't until Olivia entered my life so suddenly that I understood this.

The kiss in Olivia's hallway was meant to act as a truce. It started well, as I had imagined in my love-struck mind, but the result was disappointing at best. She's a little more feisty and determined than I gave her credit for, but in a surprising twist, I love that about her too. I have to rethink how I'm going to approach her. She and I belong together, and I have to learn to not think of Olivia in terms of what women have been to me in my past. She is right on that count, and I've proven to her and myself that she is different. Different in so many ways.

I descend the stairs to the main floor of the apartment to meet up with Carl. I mention that it would be best if he were not in the apartment during the showing as it tends to make the prospective buyers uncomfortable. He nods in his expected way.

"There is a fresh pot of coffee made, and mugs are in the cupboard beside the sink," he says while he puts on his shoes and hat. "How long do you think the viewing will last? Send me a text when you're done."

"Thanks for the coffee. I imagine we'd need about a half-hour for the viewing. Sometimes it's quick, and other times the clients linger while they discuss it with me."

Carl nods, grabs his jacket, and leaves. It would have been better to show this apartment while the sun was shining as the southwest exposure offers superb natural light, but the rain and

139

The Art of Love in New York City
overcast skies are out of my control.

I pull out three coffee mugs and search the countertop for the sugar bowl while I wait for the clients to arrive. My fingers itch to text Olivia while I wait, but I know better than to bother her further today. She told me she needs space, and as much as I'm fighting to give it to her, I have to respect her needs. She knows now that I have resolved my issues with what transpired at the awards event and that I'm a fucking schmuck for reacting the way I did.

The buzzer from street level rings out at the front door, and I answer by pressing the intercom. "Todd? Carina? Come on up." I glance over the space, adjust my tie, and remind myself of all the things that make this apartment special. Within three minutes, Todd and Carina are at the threshold while I stand waiting to shake their hands.

The showing goes well. They need the extra space that the second floor offers for their three kids. Not many New York spaces have a combined upper and lower unit or the airier rooms offered here. Their only disappointment was with the need for modernization. If they have the kind of coin I think they do, then they can afford to make the upgrades I overheard them discussing with each other.

I'm finding myself feeling a bit anxious. As much as I want to sell this apartment to the first people I show it to, that is rarely the case. The clients linger for a bit, looking out of the living room window and chatting before they shake my hand and promise to let me know later today if they decide to make an offer. "I doubt you'll find anything comparable in this area for your family's needs, but if you want to keep looking, I have two other listings that we can set appointments for later this week."

Once the clients have left, I decide to have a snoop around on the upper floor where Olivia spends the bulk of her time. At the second-floor landing on the right side is Olivia's studio.

The door is half-closed and creeks a little as I open it. I remind myself to tell Carl to oil the door hinges as the creaking makes the apartment sound old and in disrepair.

As Olivia stated, the wave sculpture she was working on is nowhere in sight. But as my eyes wander over to her easel, I see four sketches of something she's working on.

The charcoal drawings look hurried and appear to be the same object but from different perspectives. It isn't immediately clear to me what she's sketching, and so I move on to once again view the paintings she has lined up against the wall. They should all be displayed in a gallery somewhere. Why any artist with her talent only works with one gallery is surprising, but the quirks of artists are many.

I leave the studio and wander into her bedroom. During the showing and my initial viewing of the apartment, I had a quick glimpse of her personal space, but I'd not delved into the depths of what is in here. Her taste is elegant and sophisticated, much like her. I slip open a few drawers of her dresser, and in doing so, I find her collection of lingerie. Each piece is a soft pink color except for one— a black corset with lace and white accents. I touch the fabric and imagine her wearing it for me. Her smooth, long legs leading up to the high cut trim on the front, the curve that accentuates her waist, and the half cup push-up bra that may not cover her nipples have the allure of a Victorian corset. The temptation to hold it in my hands gives me a rise. I shut the drawer slowly and pray that she will come back to me one day, and I'll see her in this sexy number.

My phone vibrates in my pocket to remind me of another appointment I have later this morning. I pull out my phone, text Harjit to let her know I'm ready and set my phone ringer volume back up now that this showing is over. The only thing I know for certain about the rest of my day is that Olivia's sexy as fuck corset is never going to leave my mind and will be a titillating source for a little self-pleasuring later tonight.

The Art of Love in New York City

While Harjit drives me to my next appointment, I text Olivia this message: "Why don't you let me find you an apartment to rent. I do that as a service for my clients as well."

Her reply comes back almost immediately. "Thanks, Max, but I don't want you to know where I'm going to be living. I need my space. Please let me have it."

"For six months?"

"We'll see, Max."

I toss my phone on the seat beside me and scrub my face with my hands.

I can't wait six months for her to decide if I'm worthy of her time. "Fuck!" I say, and Harjit gives me a concerned look from her rearview mirror. "Sorry, I'm just frustrated," I say apologetically.

"I see that. What's the problem, boss? Dr. Harjit is in the house," she says, trying to make me relax.

"Women. They want you, and then they don't want you. I mean, shit," I say, running my palm over my stubbled chin again. "I made one fucking mistake."

"Yes, but it was a big one from what I hear," she says, as my car comes to a screeching halt.

"What's going on?" I ask as I peer over the seat to see why we stopped so short.

"Nothing. The jackass in front of us stopped short, and I was busy looking at your sorry ass in the rearview." Harjit gives me a cheeky grin then goes back to jostling my car through traffic.

"You're a woman," I start to say.

"Last I checked," she replies, smirking at me.

"In my haste and in the heat of feeling betrayed, I called Olivia a flake," I mutter. "How am I supposed to recover from that?"

"You can't. She has to recover from that, Max. And if she loves you the way I think she does, she will forgive you. Don't be so pushy. A woman like Olivia is worth the wait, but I think you already know this."

"I offered to help her find a rental apartment while she waits for hers to sell. She told me that she doesn't want me to know where she's moving. What the fuck am I supposed to do with that information?"

Harjit shakes her head at me and sighs loudly. "Listen, Max. Calling any artist of Olivia's caliber a flake is the ultimate insult. I can't imagine she is taking that one lightly. And for the record, you're an idiot. Having said that, I think Olivia is still in love with you and will forgive you your insult because I know you didn't mean it – not to her anyway – but, you know, it's gonna take some time."

"How did you know that was the problem?" I ask, curious to find out who's talking about my personal life.

"I have moles in the office," she says and smirks.

"Great," I mumble into my fist at the edge of my jaw as I look out the window to the pedestrians at the crosswalk. I nod in acceptance of Harjit's advice. "I know I fucked up, that I'm hot-headed when it comes to trust, and I am feeling very much the idiot you say I am. Jesus, this whole thing just pisses me off. I can't wait six months for her to forgive me, Harjit." I grab my phone back off the leather seat at my right and check for messages. Nothing further from Olivia, but that doesn't surprise me.

143

Chapter 28 – Olivia

As much as my life is moving backward from where I thought it would be heading, I'm hopeful that this move to Bed-Stuy is a good one. The rental apartment is the size of my current studio space in its entirety, but I'll find a way to make this major downsizing workable.

It is only for six months, or until our apartment is sold. I should have asked Max how the showing went, but I'll let Carl make the inquiries and hear any news second-hand through him. I can't see or hear from Max without my heart twisting in my chest.

I realize I'm selfish, but I have too many other things to worry about. I have to make arrangements for a moving truck, possibly put a few of my things in storage, find out from my lawyer when my first alimony check is to arrive, among other things. I also want to secure the art supplies I need for the big sculpture, and I'm hopeful that won't break my monthly budget before I've even moved into the rental.

A message appears on my phone from Teddy. "Lunch today?"

"Yes. Where? When?

"I'll pick you up at one o'clock."

When Teddy arrives in her limo, I am waiting on the sidewalk out front of my building. Nathanial, her driver, exits the limo swiftly to open the door for me. As I slip inside, Teddy is all smiles and looks like a million dollars in her all-black sleeveless jumpsuit. "Love the outfit," I say. Combined with her long black hair styled in loose waves that cascade over her right shoulder and her trademark red pouty lips, she is a vision to behold.

"Donna Karen," she replies and winks at me. "You look fresh and pretty, and edible. Can I eat you first and then go for lunch?"

My eyes pop, and my mouth goes agape. I press my finger over my lips and make a shushing sound as I wonder if Nathanial can hear our conversation. Teddy catches my concern and laughs. "He only hears what he needs to hear. Isn't that right, Nate?"

"Yes, Ms. Braithwaite."

"You see. Perfectly safe to say what you want," she says as she reaches forward to squeeze my knee. "Now, answer the question."

I settle back into my seat and smile at Teddy. "You need to give a girl a little more warning. I've only got enough time to have lunch today. Can I have a raincheck on the date?"

"Of course, Olivia. "I just needed to see your pretty face and share a laugh or two."

Later in the afternoon, the rain tapers off, and I take this opportunity to go for a run. The humidex is in the seventy percent range, but I need the run to clear my head of thoughts of Max.

Upon arriving back to the apartment from my lunch date with Teddy, I find Carl sitting in his chair in the living room reading today's paper. "Any good news, or is it the same negative shit as always?" I ask as I pass behind him on my way to the main bathroom.

"There's nothing worth repeating, that's for damned sure." Carl rests the paper on his lap and looks over to me. "The showing went well. Max thinks their interest was high. We'll see, I guess," he says, then picks his paper back up and flips over to the next page.

The Art of Love in New York City

The rustling of the newsprint in his hands is such a familiar one to me, and that makes me wonder what other sounds I might miss when we completely part ways. The scritch of his slippers sliding across the hardwood floor, the tinkling of his spoon in his coffee and teacups after he stirs in his sugar, the soft chuckle he makes when he's amused, albeit he rarely laughs now, and the way he clears his throat intermittently throughout the day; all those things are little, insignificant, but they are the things that remind me of Carl.

I walk into the bathroom and take off my dress. I place it in the laundry basket before heading upstairs to my bedroom to get my jogging clothes.

Carl's eyes follow me as I parade past him in my underwear and bra. "Don't look if you don't plan to touch," I say. I should have kept that thought to myself since I know he's not interested. It makes me wonder what does interest him anymore. It sure as shit ain't me.

When I reach my bedroom, I start to dig through my t-shirt drawer and notice one of the drawers on my dresser is not fully closed. I'm sure I closed all of them when I did my clean-up before the showing. "Those clients of Max's had better not been going through my belongings," I mutter. Never mind. I probably didn't close that drawer properly in my hurry to clean up. My mind is all over the place as of late.

I head out the door of my apartment building and do a bit of a jog on the spot while I shake out my shoulders and arms before I begin my run. Janine exits from the lobby just as I'm prepping for my run and begins a quick chat with me. Once again, I'm invited for coffee, and I agree to do that later tonight after dinner. I'll tell her about Carl and me, and that I'm moving next weekend during our visit tonight.

We part ways with a wave, and I head out down the sidewalk toward the park in a light running pace. I get two blocks down the road when I spot Max's car taking the corner across the street from the coffee shop. I quickly turn the sidewalk corner to get out of his possible line of sight and then stop at the front of the church to catch my breath. I'd forgotten how much harder it is to run in this level of humidity. Maybe I should walk for a while and forget about running today.

I don't know why Max would be driving down my street unless he has an appointment with Carl that Carl didn't bother to tell me about. I debate in my head if I should turn back to figure that out, but that would mean I'd have to see Max's handsome face again, and I can't do that yet. I can't let him distract me from my plans.

It dawns on me that I never mentioned to Olivia that my brother, Russell owns the loft apartment I showed her and made love to her in. It makes me laugh to think that she might think I'd feel it was okay to have sex in a random client's apartment during a showing. I should have told her back then who owned the unit, and I have to wonder if she thinks poorly of me because of what I let happen between us there. Hopefully, that thought never crossed her mind. I shake my head and remind myself that I could micro analyze everything I've said and done to her and drive myself crazy, worrying that something other than the one insult in my office is what made her walk away from us. I have to stop thinking about her, but I'm not sure how I'm supposed to do that.

My afternoon meeting with the team at the office begins at three o'clock. Harjit gets me to the office ten minutes before the meeting begins. I shoot a couple of ounces of bourbon down my throat, gather my papers, and head into the boardroom.

We've gotten some significant increases in buyers and sellers looking to hire us since our top sales award win. We plastered ads all over New York in any trade magazine, newspaper and online format we could get into before deadline, touting our superior sales record at a cost I don't want to know, but it is worth it to strike while the iron is hot.

I tried to keep my ears tuned to the voices in the room, but my mind repeatedly wandered to thoughts of Olivia. She's not only upset with me; she's struggling to find her ground. I'm going to do as she asked and let her breathe for a few weeks. Maybe by then, she'll be more receptive to talking to me.

"You with us here?" Clint asks.

"Sorry, what?"

"Did you hear that the interest rate is going up in the next week? We have clients sitting on the fence, and if they need financing, we should call them all to remind them to secure mortgages before the rate increases."

"Oh, yes. Good idea. Who do we have undecided?"

Clint slides over six file folders to me and nods. Those are the ones you have worked with directly. There are five more here that I've been talking with in the past week. Should we call them all first thing tomorrow morning?" he asks.

"Yes. Perfect." I stack the folders neatly in front of me and glance at the faces around the table. "Is there anything else we need to discuss?" My team looks at me a bit strangely, and I realize I'm not paying attention. A round of noes, nopes, and I'm goods reply to me. "Right. Back to work then."

While I gather up my paperwork and head back to my desk, I remember Olivia mentioning that she had two smaller sculptures that she'd brought to the Lipinski Gallery a few weeks ago. I make a mental note to visit the Lipinski website to view them. If Olivia doesn't want to see me, and I know she's shy on cash, the least I can do is support her art and buy one or both of those pieces. I'll give Harjit the money to purchase the pieces, so Olivia isn't aware that I had anything to do with it.

Later that afternoon, I invite a few of the top-selling agents in my office for drinks at the pub tonight. We decide to pile into my car and have Harjit drive us there before she heads home for the night. I was downing my fifth Bourbon on the rocks when the bitch from hell sauntered near our table. "Don't even think about it," I said as loud as I could to be sure Kelsey didn't stop at our table to chat with any of the other agents. I'm feeling brave with myself after a few strong cocktails, and she isn't getting near me if I can help it. My comment only proved to be an invitation to her, and I should have known better.

"What did you say?" Kelsey stops dead and turns to freeze me with her cold as ice eyes.

"I said, don't even think about it, but what I really meant to say was get the fuck away from me, you conniving cunt, but you know, I'm too polite to say that in public." I can't help myself and break out into a full belly laugh. A few of my agents give me a shocked look, but they are all well aware of what Kelsey did to me. However, they've never seen me at my worst in front of her or know that she kissed my lover in an attempt to sabotage my relationship with Olivia.

"You don't deserve someone like Olivia," she says, attempting to make me feel bad. "You deserve never to find true love, and I hope she leaves your sorry ass before she finds out who you really are, Max." Kelsey's stance widens, she locks her arms over her chest, and a smirk forms over her dark red painted lips.

"Walk away, Kelsey, before everyone can hear the devil himself calling out for his mistress." I toss the last of my fifth bourbon down my throat and rise to leave for the men's room. I don't need to hang around just for her and me to throw knives at each other. And I'm better than this. I need to learn how to ignore her as if she didn't exist when she's in my presence. It is the only way to deal with her moving forward. I risk my reputation calling her out in public places. This only reminds me of Olivia and how she gave me that disapproving look when Kelsey approached us at the Bistro.

I return from the restroom and gather my coat. I apologize for my sharp tongue and slipping out early but promise to pay the full tab for the crew for tonight. I hand my server my credit card for a running tab and head home. Once again, I've let Kelsey ruin my night.

Kelsey's harsh words about love spur me on to post a little something sweet on Twitter intended for Olivia to read: *"It is so damned sexy when you are silly and laughing with each other one minute, then so ready to make love the next."*

On the way home, I tweet one more time. Mostly because I'm feeling my drinks and because I'm desperate to make Olivia connect with me in any way possible. Even a like on my romantic tweets would be enough for me to know we're still together. *"I'd live each day to the fullest but without you that's not possible."*

It has been three weeks since Olivia told me she needed her space. She should have completed her move to her new rental space by now, and I'm still sending Clint out for showings at her apartment twice a week. We've had good feedback on the location and the uniqueness of the space, however, none of the clients have put pen to paper for an offer. I'll arrange for a second marketing blitz directed at real estate agents in this area for that apartment in hopes that it will find the right buyer soon. Carl is opposed to having an open house, as many clients do; therefore, I have to be more creative in getting other realtors' interest piqued to show it to their clients. A split commission is better than no commission.

Harjit came back to the office this afternoon with both of the smaller sculptures Olivia created. I'll keep the elephant palm leaf piece and give the coral reef cluster piece to Russell and Nadine for their upcoming fifth wedding anniversary gift. Nadine will love it.

I've had quite a few sleepless nights lately. I miss Olivia more than I imagined I would. I want to text her to see if she's doing okay in her new place, but I'm concerned about her thinking I'm stalking her. She has not posted recently on Twitter, but I imagine her busy life and all the changes she's going through don't allow her much

The Art of Love in New York City
downtime.

While I kick my feet up on my coffee table in my usual TV viewing position, I set my phone beside me, then adjust my popcorn bowl over my lap and turn on the movie channel. As I'm flicking through the options that are growing thin since I've already viewed most of these films, my cell phone vibrates with a text message. To my surprise, it is from Olivia.

"You shouldn't have, and thank you." I fumble with my phone in my hands with my butter greased fingers while I figure out what to reply to her. "How did you know it was me and you're welcome."

"I was in the gallery having lunch with Sasha when Harjit came to pick them up. Nice try on attempting to hide behind Harjit for the purchases."

I laugh to myself. "Bad timing on Harjit's part. I should have had her put on a blond wig and dress differently."

"She's a good sport, Max, but I doubt she'd have played along with the idea of a disguise. Anyway, I appreciate the gesture."

I pause texting while I take a drink of my soda and think of a way to make sure she doesn't end this conversation too quickly. "How are you? Are you okay in your rental?"

"Yes. It's tiny, but I'll manage. It's only for a short while. Any news on a potential buyer for the apartment? I haven't spoken to Carl in over a week."

"I'm doing another marketing blitz to realtors I know who have clients that frequently purchase in your area. That usually works well to spark new interest."

"Good to know. If it takes six months to sell, that will be fine, but I hope for a sale quickly. I'd love to buy the loft space you showed me, but I'm sure that listing is sold by now."

"It's still available. I never told you, but that is Russell and Nadine's old apartment. They rented it out for the first year after they moved, thinking they might come back to New York at some point, but now they've agreed to stay in LA permanently."

"I wish you'd have told me that before. Would they wait for me to sell my place so I can take it off their hands?"

Now I'm excited. This is what my plan was all along. I broached the subject with Russell when we were in LA about him lowering the price because I had an interested party, but they could not come up as high as he was asking. He hummed and hawed over it, then gave me the okay to drop the price by fifty grand.

"Are you one-hundred percent sure you want the loft?"

"YES!" she texts back in full caps.

"Okay, okay...stop yelling. Lol. I'll give Russell a down payment to take it off the market, so it doesn't get sold before you are ready to take it. Is it okay for me to do that for you?" It's a few minutes before Olivia decides.

"Can I use my commission from the sale of the two pieces you bought? How much of a deposit does he need to hold it for me?"

"Keep your commission, Olivia. I'll convince Russell to take it off the market while we wait for your apartment to sell. He'll be pissed at me for asking, but I'm sure he'll agree because it's you."

"You go out on too many limbs for me, Max. I can't let you do that to him. Thank you, but no."

How did I know she'd turn me down? Olivia isn't one to take gifts easily. And I'm guessing she would feel obligated to me on a level that makes her uncomfortable.

The Art of Love in New York City

"You are willing to let your stubborn streak make you possibly lose out on the perfect loft?"

"So now I'm a flake and stubborn? Geez, Max. You sure know how to sweet talk a woman."

"Don't do that, Olivia. You know I'm eternally regretting saying that to you, of all people. I'm in love with you."

Another few minutes pass as she mulls over my last text. Did I press her too hard into thinking that she has to tell me she loves me too? Dammit. I can't help but regret telling her this. I toss my phone to my side and scrub my stubbled face with my palms. I'm tired, anxious, and heartbroken. A few minutes later, my phone vibrates again with her reply.

"I'm confused about my feelings for you, Max. I won't deny that you mean the world to me, but I'm worried that what you and I have shared in the past was a rebound for me. It happened so quickly after Carl and I decided to part ways. It doesn't mean that I don't love you. It just means I'm not ready."

I let out a long breath as I reread her message. The good news is that she feels the same way. The bad news is that she's still holding back. I fucking need her in my life more than I ever thought I'd need a woman. It's like a part of me was missing before she came into my life, and I'm only recognizing that now. I send her three small words.

"I need you."

"Explain need."

"Do you want a report on how many times I masturbate at the thought of you? That photo I took of you in the loft bathroom brings me so much pleasure. Just you texting me has given me an erection. That is what I mean by the word need."

She makes me wait a long few minutes before she replies. I'm dying here waiting for her message to appear. The dots on my screen dance while I take another sip of my soda and turn my TV off.

"Show me."

Alright. This is a first. I've never sent a dick pic to anyone, but if that's what my girl wants, that's what my girl gets. I rise from the couch to close the drapes on my windows, then drop my pants and underwear. Should I take the picture standing up or lying down? Fuck me, I can't decide. I resolve to lie down on the couch and take the shot from an elevated perspective. I can't help but laugh as I review the image.

"Are you asking me for a dick pic? I'm hard as fuck for you."

"Yes. Prove to me that you're hard."

I send the picture, but don't comment. I can only imagine what she's thinking or planning on texting me.

"Mmm. I do miss that particular part of your body."

"Your turn to show me some skin," I reply and smirk. She won't oblige me, but it never hurts to ask. Seconds later, I get a shot of her ample cleavage through her open blouse.

"Such a tease. I want more skin than that, Olivia."

"What's your fantasy, Max?"

"You, straddled over me wearing that black corset number in your dresser."

"I knew someone had been through my drawers! Max, you are a bad boy."

"Put it on for me and take a picture of yourself. I'm dying to see you in it."

"Give me a few minutes."

I think my dick just got harder if that were even possible. Now that I'm half-naked lying on my couch, I may as well get completely naked and pull off my shirt, then lie back down while she takes the image I asked for. I want so badly to pleasure myself while I wait for her to text me again. I will myself to wait, and I gotta admit to myself how real this struggle is. I check the time on my phone and note it has only been three minutes.

I need a distraction, so I click my TV back on to something boring like the news. This relaxes me a bit until I try to move and realize my skin is stuck to the leather. I need a towel or a blanket or something to put underneath me.

Once I get myself organized and think about other things, my hardon subsides a little. But the moment I hear my phone vibrate, I'm fully aroused again. Those dots. Those fucking dots dance as my patience wears thin. Then, there it is. "Holy fuck!" I say aloud. I drop my ass on the couch and fist myself as I gaze at the sexiest shot of Olivia I could ever have imagined. Her curvy frame and all those perfect parts that I've had the pleasure of tasting are accentuated by the cut and style of the corset. I know that if I ever get the chance to physically touch her while she's in it, it will very quickly end up on the floor, but the visual is killer. She lays on her side, her hair pooling in soft waves over her shoulder, her breasts spilling tantalizingly out of the push-up cups just as I hoped they would when I held the garment in my hands in her bedroom. Her lips are slightly parted, painted bright red to match the detail on the corset, and I swear her eyes are watching me lose myself as I stare at her image. I want her in that corset as much as I want her out of it.

My hand strokes my shaft slowly, and as much as I want to close my eyes and focus on the movement of my hand, I cannot take my eyes off her image. She is my kryptonite, my goddess, my one true love. I don't know how long I was sitting there, slowly stroking myself, cloaked in a shroud of sexual ecstasy, but another message from Olivia pops up under her image.

"Did you get it? Do you like it?"

The widest fucking grin lifts my cheeks to new heights, and my eyes start to water at the thought she worried I didn't get it or that I wasn't already getting myself off looking at it. I'm emotional, not just aroused. I stop for a second to reply.

"I swear you are trying to kill me. Tell me you are lying on the bed, that your hand is between those amazing fucking legs and you are using your sweet wetness to pleasure yourself."

At that moment, after I sent her that last text, I decide to go the full distance with this sexting. I prop my phone up on the coffee table and hit the video button. She's going to witness what she does to me. I hit the record button and slide my ass up on the edge of my leather couch nice and close to the phone. I start to stroke myself again, fisting a little tighter, using long, firm strokes lubricated by my precum, then gradually increase my pace until I come all over myself and my hand in spurts like a volcano erupting. I'd never, in a million years, thought I'd ever jack off on video for any reason, but she took me there in seconds flat.

I don't bother to review the video before I send it off to Olivia. It speaks for itself. I follow it up with this message.

"I warned you to be careful with how you wield your power over me. I need to touch you, kiss you, and taste you. Stop denying me. I don't know how much longer I can live without you. Tell me where you are, and I'll be there as soon as possible."

As expected, Olivia goes silent on me. I should have known making demands to her was pointless, but I'm tired of waiting for her to come to her senses. I rise from the couch to clean myself up and shake my head before I take a good long look at my reflection in the vanity mirror. I'm so fucked. I return to the living room to redress, knowing that what we shared these past few minutes is over. My phone vibrates again as I zip up my jeans, and to my surprise, Olivia has returned a video of her face as she comes at the thought of me. Her soft moans, her eyes rolling into the back of her head, her short quick breaths just seconds before she releases makes me hard as steel again.

I replay the video multiple times, and I can't help myself from dropping my jeans again and re-enacting my self-pleasuring over watching her come while still wearing that gorgeous corset. And I was right. Her nipples are not covered by the half-cup push-up bra. Her nipples are peaked high, tight and deep rosy pink. My mouth salivates at the vision of me sucking on them while I watch her pleasure herself as I lean over her on my hands and knees. It is one thing to watch porn videos and get aroused, but when it is the woman you love sending you this stuff, your heart stops short of stroking out from beating too fast in your chest. But that's how I know I'm in love. No other woman could do this to me, not like this. Nobody but Olivia has that power.

Chapter 30 – Olivia

I'm overcome with desire while I wrestle with my decision to keep my distance from Max. I was steadfast in my objective. But after this sexting event, watching him come for me at my simple gesture of sending him a photograph of myself, I resolve to show him how much the thought of him gives me pleasure in a reciprocated video. The mind has no clarity when it is sexually stimulated.

This is what teenagers do on their computers, not grown assed adults, but here we are letting sex control common sense regardless of our maturity. And I don't regret it.

I should give Max my address, but that would mean abandoning the purpose of my forced distancing from him. Part of me wants to stop being selfish, and the other part of me is still directionless. This tiny rental apartment feels like a womb, where I can hide to heal my wounds and grow into a new and improved Olivia. Until I'm fully reborn, I cannot let Max or anyone else know where I am. I send him a new text message.

"I'm sorry, Max. I'm not ready to tell you where to find me. My desires and love for you have not faltered, and after tonight I think you know this."

" I am not a patient man, but for you, I will wait. Just know that this is torture to me."

My heart breaks a little more after his last text. I know I should reply to him, but there will be more conversation on the subject if I do. I resort to re-watching his video, and it only serves to make me put my greedy fingers between my legs once again. I reach inside my side table drawer for my vibrator, and in my mind, I envision my hand is Max's. His fingers ease my dampness for him over my sex in long slow strokes while he whispers words drenched in erotic prose to me between tender kisses. I move my hips up and down to aid in this stroking while my clit becomes engorged with need. My breasts feel fuller, and my breaths come short and quick in anticipation. I'm as wet as I'm going to be as I slip the vibrating rabbit sex toy into position, sink the dildo inside of myself, and feel the little massaging prongs around my thundering clit. It is almost too much to bear. I come so quickly it astonishes me while my legs squeeze tight around my pulsing sex toy and my hands. Tears form at the corner of my eyes when I realize how much I miss his touch.

This is a struggle for us both, and I need to solve my issues sooner than later. Reaching for my cell phone beside me on my bed, I send Max one last text tonight.

"This is torture for me too."

My art supplies for the larger sculpture are to arrive this morning, and I'm excited to begin working on it. With my sketches clipped to the easel, I sip my coffee, reviewing them while I wait for the sun to warm the inside of my little space, and I can fully imagine the completed piece in my head. This is positive, and for the first time in weeks, I feel in control.

The buzzer on my door tells me the art supplies have arrived. I make room next to the easel for the boxes by shoving aside the paint cabinet on wheels to the left by two feet. This little womb I've decided to live in temporarily is swiftly becoming an oven as the sun fully encompasses the windows. I plug in my portable air conditioner before answering the door and signing the shipping documents. Thankfully, the delivery guy agreed to wheel his hand-truck with the clay-filled boxes over to my work area, but only after I begged him nicely, gave him a sweet smile, and offered him a twenty-dollar tip for the ten seconds of inconvenience.

This is it. The moment I've been waiting for. My hands move fast across the tops of the clay boxes to open them with my scissors.

The warm sun filling my art space, my excitement to begin building the largest sculpture I've ever attempted, and the lack of any distractions fills my heart with hope that I'll master my vision of the two waves connecting in a lover's dance – baile folklorico style. Perhaps once I've completed it, I'll have the perfect name for it. In the meantime, in my head, I'm calling it El Baile (The Dance).

The prep work involved is a more significant task than it usually is since my workspace is in a new setting, and this piece is much larger than I'm used to creating. I've placed the clay in the sun below my window to soften it up while I get prepared. I struggle with the time involved to get organized as I am impatient to get my hands dirty. I remind myself that the prep work is an essential stage of creativity to help tamper down my anxiety. Within half an hour, I'm ready to place my first slab of clay upon my work surface, and I breathe a sigh of relief when my fingers feel the warm, softened medium in my hands.

My easel with my sketches sits directly in front of my workspace, and in my mind, I envision the base of the sculpture and how broad it needs to be for stability. It amazes me how quickly my clay supplies dwindle as block after block of the warmed medium gets applied. I found myself needing to draw the sheer drapes across the window as the sun's heat was making the sculpture prematurely dry out. I have to continually spritz the sculpture with water to keep it moist and pliable while my wave vision comes to life.

Now that I have the basic form, it is time to wrap it up in plastic. I need to take a break to have a bite to eat and rest my arms. I get so lost in my work that I often don't realize how many hours have passed. I am meticulous in wrapping the plastic around the sculpture as I don't want to repeat what happened to the last one.

The Art of Love in New York City

While I take a quick breather to relax and make something to eat, I scan my Twitter account on my laptop for the latest tweets that I've missed. I find a few from Max that are new between the political views, other artists' work, and joke tweets. He is focused on his business, as expected, but he's tweeted a few romantic things lately, and I have to wonder if they are meant for me to read, regardless of them being public postings. My ego gets a small lift at the prospect that they are.

Much like myself, Max is driven by a passion for his work, and that is one of the many things I find attractive about him. I click on his profile image to enlarge it, then lean back in my kitchen chair to admire him. I mumble to myself, "What am I going to do about you, Max." I kiss my fingers and touch his image on my screen while I attempt to tamp down my welling emotions.

Chapter 31 – Max

It has been another two weeks since Olivia has been in contact with me. I decide to post another romantic message hoping that she will see it and understand it is meant for her. *"I've found somebody to love. You should too...but not her. She's mine."*

I chanced a visit to Sasha's gallery in hopes that Olivia might be there or that Sasha could give me an update on how Olivia is doing. I'd forgotten that the gallery was closed for August while Sasha and her husband took holidays. Olivia continues to ghost me no matter how many times I try to engage her on Twitter or send her texts to her phone. I'm becoming more frustrated by the day, and I don't know how much longer I can take this separation.

My cell phone vibrates to remind me of a meeting I've arranged for one o'clock this afternoon. The prospective client is a friend of my biggest client, Dr. Madson. I am to meet them at the client's home, and as I climb back into my car with Harjit at my ready, I give her the address and trust that we will arrive at the appointment on time.

Teddy is not commonly a woman's name, and thus I was quite surprised when she greeted me at the door to shake my hand and introduce herself. She is a tall, slender, raven-haired woman who holds herself with a level of confidence that could make many men feel weak in her presence. I'm not one of those men, and as a potential client, I need her to understand that I'm not weak – that isn't my style. Yet, her need to be in control should not be neglected. It's a give-and-take situation that I'm quite familiar with after so many years in the business. If she is as astute as my first impression has given me, she'll have already picked up on my confident energy. I enter the opulent top floor apartment and am swiftly handed a Champaign glass by her assistant, then led down the white marbled floor hall to a grand space flooded with light through a long wall of floor to ceiling windows. Every surface in the home is white, and it gives me the impression I've walked into the waiting room for Heaven. I've seen homes with this stark decorating scheme several times, and one will either love it or hate it. It has to be done right so as not to make one feel cold and swallowed by the décor. The only offer of colour is in the vibrance of the large tropical plants and floral arrangements. The softness of the lines of the furniture, the plush area rugs juxtaposed against the cold white marble floors, and the billowing sheer drapes in the hot summer wind by the expansive balcony, combine to make me hear angels singing in my head.

"This is quite spectacular," I say as Teddy seats herself comfortably on the overstuffed, diamond tufted white fabric-covered couch. There are several references to the Fleur de Lis in this space, which makes me wonder if Teddy is of French descent.

My first question when I meet new clients is to inquire how long they've been living here. Teddy's smile is genuine as she sets her champagne glass down on the coffee table before her. "Just a few years. I had no intention of selling so quickly, but I came across a spectacular apartment that is nearing completion overlooking Central Park, and I couldn't resist snapping it up."

I nod, but now I am curious why she wouldn't have hired the same realtor who sold her the new apartment to sell her existing residence. Something must have gone wrong for her in that deal for her to seek a different agent to represent her sale. "Have you listed this property before meeting with me?"

"Yes. Well. You see, I was convinced by the agent who sold me the Central Park apartment to let him market this one. However, he kept beating me down on the price point for the sale, and I'd had enough of his lowballing. I know what this apartment is worth based on others sold in this tower. I refuse to list my home at a lower price than what other apartments have sold for here to expedite a quick sale. To be clear, Max, I don't need a quick sale."

"Thank you for your honesty. It is imperative that we are upfront with each other to have a successful business arrangement. And, what number do you have that is your best and final?"

"I couldn't sell for less than eight million," Teddy states matter-of-factly.

I nod in agreement. "There have been four sales in this tower in the past year. All of them have been sold in a matter of three months from their initial date of listing and for close to their asking price. The market is stable now, and I don't feel as though that will change soon. With that in mind, we should list somewhere around eight point three."

Teddy's smile widens as she reaches for her champagne glass on the coffee table. "And at that asking price, how long do you think it would take to complete a sale?"

"I cannot predict the future, Teddy, but I'm confident we will have a good interest here. The views are stunning, the décor is exceptional, and this tower's location is highly sought after. Would you like to give me a tour?"

Teddy nods, and just then, her assistant enters the grand room to hand me the floorplan layout of the apartment and the original sale documents when Teddy purchased it. "That's perfect. Thank you."

After our tour of the apartment is completed, Teddy invites me to join her for dinner. I'm taken aback by the offer, but I have no other plans and accept without hesitation.

We part ways, and I agree to return with the listing documents and enjoy dinner with her at seven tonight.

I seem to have found myself in an interesting situation with Teddy. She and I have shared multiple dinners, some concerning business, and others very casual as if we were on a date. I like her company, but I still feel obligated to Olivia regardless of my attraction to Teddy and her obvious attraction to me. We laugh easily; we share many of the same interests, and what's not to love about dating a woman with her kind of wealth?

Our fourth date was back inside her apartment. Her chef prepared the most brilliant Indian Lamb Biryani meal I've ever tasted. The wine flowed a little too freely, and I found myself needing to taste something more than just good food and expensive wine. My urges flood to the surface, my ego well intact and ready to show Teddy that I have more to offer than conversation tonight. The question is will she be open to my advances.

In my drunken state, I'd all but forgotten my self-imposed devotion to Olivia, but I've given all the time I can manage to wait for her to come to her senses. Maybe this is the point where I move on. Teddy's eyes meet mine while her chef clears our dishes from the table and refills our wine glasses. A slow growing, almost bashful smile eases over her lips, and I know what she's thinking.

I rise from my chair and reach for her hand. Our eyes remain focused on each other as she stands before me, inches from my body. I lean in, state my intentions with a gentle kiss, and pray my gesture is taken as intended, however, she may think I'm simply thanking her for the outstanding meal and company. Teddy reciprocates without hesitation. For a brief moment, I feel guilty for letting my lips grace that of any woman that isn't Olivia, but that moment passes the longer I hold Teddy's lips against mine.

Her hand firmly planted on my growing erection sends me the

signal that I wanted without asking. She slides the heel of her palm with purpose up and down my firm shaft beneath my bursting zipper, and if that isn't a signal for fuck me, I don't know what is.

I pull Teddy's mouth tighter to mine with my hand around the back of her neck, and she bites my lips. The sounds of the chef clearing up his workstation behind us stop us from progressing this tease in his company. Teddy's fingers weave between mine as she leads me down the hall toward her bedroom. I close the door tight behind me, and before I've turned back around to face her, she has slipped off her blouse and locked her eyes on mine. Words are not necessary for me to understand what Teddy wants from me, and so in the silence, we undress and dive into another heady kiss.

There is a seductiveness about Teddy that would draw any red-blooded man into her web. She's not a woman of classic beauty, not like Olivia is, but there is no denying Teddy's appeal to the opposite sex. Her long black hair, a penetrating stare that cannot be ignored, a fit trim body and her full red lips are a stamp of a woman who knows she is powerful, and all combine to make a clear statement of her intent to lure you in. But for all her bold appearance and clear wealth, she is surprisingly approachable.

Teddy invited me to a private party hosted by her father at his palatial home this Friday evening. Teddy's driver will pick me up at my apartment then swing back to her place to collect her.

I scan my closet for my most expensive suits, as I'm desperate to make the best impression on whoever is attending. Having my foot in the door to a collection of uber-wealthy people can only make my business more profitable. However, I'll need to be discrete in my approach. Based on Teddy's conversation with me earlier, my take on the attendees is that her father is influential in several business categories, including stock trading, tech & even agriculture. These are the people who have money to burn. They love to buy and sell real estate and boast about their latest property acquisitions with each other while in the same breath complaining about the cost of gardeners for their massive properties.

We arrive at the gated residence owned by her family for over seventy years and are greeted at the door by a stern-looking gentleman who would likely die before cracking a smile. "Don't mind Mr. Adamson," Teddy whispers in my ear as we pass through the grand entry doors into a three-story high foyer. "He's a tough nut to crack and rarely smiles, but my father and he get along famously. Mr. Adamson has been our butler since long before I was born."

As my eyes follow the ceiling height down the tall, ornately detailed plaster columns supporting a magnificent marble double staircase. I admire the heavy wood doors that lead from one parlor room to the next as I have to take a deep breath before following further into the residence. She smiles at me as I absorb the massiveness of everything my eyes land upon. "Have you never been in a home this size?" she asks, curious since my profession would make one assume otherwise.

"Yes, I have. But estates such as this are rarely on the market. Much like your family, the estates are often passed down from one generation to the next." She nods to me in agreement. As we enter the courtyard in the back of the grand home, we are greeted by a server with a choice of champagne or wine. I pass on both as I'd much rather have a bourbon on the rocks in my hand. I see to my left an open bar and give Teddy a quick peck on her cheek before pointing toward the bar and heading over to get my much-needed bourbon cocktail.

When I return to Teddy's side, the first person she introduces me to is none other than her ex-husband. In fact, she introduces me to him as such before telling me his name is Mitchell.

I try to keep my face from showing any form of shock for how casually the introduction goes, but he and Teddy must have had an amicable split. As we move along to meet others, I quirk an eyebrow at her, and she laughs at me. "Don't worry about Mitchell. Our marriage was only three years long, and we've been divorced for five years. He's no threat or the least bit jealous of any man I bring to daddy's dinner parties.

"Why is he still inside your father's circle?"

"He works for my father, supporting his tech interests. Legal counsel, predominantly." I nod and appreciate that this evening may be far more interesting than I first thought. I am mingling with some of the biggest names in New York this evening.

Teddy's father appears to have everyone who is anyone's number in his pocket, which suits me fine. Although only a handful of guests are interested in knowing what I do for a living, the ones who did inquire were receptive. I didn't hand out any business cards for fear of appearing gauche. When one of the guests asked if I had a card, I told them that Teddy would be happy to connect us should my services be required. That seemed to please Teddy as her smile for me afterward was followed by a wink.

Teddy and I return to her apartment by midnight. She offers to have me share the night with her, and I don't think twice about accepting. It has been a successful day for me, and I wouldn't mind finishing it off with a good toss of the sheets.

I seem to find myself attracted to the women who ooze confidence, but that doesn't explain Olivia. She's the only woman who has a frailness about her that I've dated and I adored that about her. It's so genuine. It is a pity that she and I couldn't make a go of it. I truly do love her.

Chapter 33 – Olivia

After four weeks of not being in touch with Sasha, I receive a call from her inviting me to lunch. She will be beside herself with what I've accomplished on the wave sculpture since she left for her annual holiday.

When I arrive at the restaurant, Sasha has already secured a table for us. She leaps from her chair to greet me and kiss my cheek. Her enthusiasm has always been one of my favourite things about her, and she makes me feel so good when I'm in her company. Sasha begins to rattle off all the things she did on her travels, and I happily listen while I sip my cocktail. Even while our meals are in front of us, she continues to talk so much that I'm done eating, and she's not consumed but half of her meal.

When a break in her conversation comes, I pop out my cell phone and show her how far along the wave sculpture is. I don't want to tell her that it's been on hold at this stage for nearly two weeks as I've run out of money to buy more art supplies, but I have to come up with an answer to that question if she poses it. "Do you like it?" I ask.

"Livie! Oh, my god, it's so big. Are you sure you're comfortable attempting such a large sculpture?" she pauses for a second before adding, "I just mean that the first time you attempted a large piece, it was, well, you know, not your best work."

I scowl at her. Not because she was gently reprimanding me for attempting such an expensive piece when I'm broke as shit, and I'd failed miserably once before, but because she reminded me of that time in my early career as a new artist in her gallery. "I don't need reminding of that time in my life, Sasha."

She nods and takes her gaze off me while she sips her drink. Then her expression changes to a pinched brow, and I have no idea what has caught her eye. "Did you and Max break up?" she asks, now looking me square in the eyes with her features softening to worry.

"Well. No. Not exactly." I fidget with my empty plate and napkin, then take a nervous sip of my drink. "I told him I needed my space while I worked on the sculpture and cleared my head of all the stress from selling the apartment and Carl divorcing me. I'm not used to being under that much pressure. Falling in love with another man within all those other things just felt untimely."

Sasha's eyes remain fixed on me. She casually plays with the straw in her cocktail glass while I explain the situation, then she looks up toward the ceiling of the restaurant, then over to the left, then over to the right, as if she's suddenly afraid to look directly at me. "What on earth are you doing?" I ask, leaning forward now that the server has removed my plate and cutlery.

"Nothing, Livie. Just thinking, that's all."

"You look like you had something in your eye and were trying to get rid of it without sticking your fingers in them," I say and giggle. "Sometimes, you do the strangest things, Sasha."

"Yes. I do love to entertain you," she says and giggles back. "So, I guess we're done with lunch? Shall we go?"

"Sure. I should get back to the studio. Oh, shit! I forgot to tell you that we have accepted an offer on the apartment. Max's agent, Jared, found a buyer. The deal is to close on the fifteenth. I'm so excited. You have no idea how much waiting for the sale of the apartment weighed me down. I feel like it was the last stronghold that Carl had on me, you know?"

Sasha nods, but her eyes keep darting from my face to something behind me.

"What are you looking at?" I would have thought that she'd

be focused solely on me with my great news, but something else has clearly captured her attention.

"Nothing!" she stammers as she grabs my hand and forces a big smile on her face. I narrow my eyes at her as I know something is not right. I attempt to turn my head to see what she was looking at, but Sasha catches my attention with a question. "Is it alright if I take care of the lunch tab? You can get it next time."

"Yes, sure. Thank you." I rise from my seat and turn to take my purse off the chair's back when Max, sitting several tables away from behind me, catches my eye. He's dining with a slender, raven-haired woman in a white dress, looking love-struck as he stares into her eyes, then plants a sensuous kiss on her lips. The longer I stare, the more I realize that the woman Max is kissing is Teddy. Are you fucking kidding me? How on earth would they know each other? I'm frozen. The restaurant suddenly turns cold while swallowing me whole in a claustrophobic way as I come to terms with the fact that Max was not waiting for me as he promised. I feel so betrayed.

Sasha catches me in my state of shock, stands before me to block my view, and asks the passing server if there is a rear exit. This is what she was looking at over my shoulder; Max is involved with Teddy.

Sasha pulls me from my frozen stance to drag me out of the restaurant before Max is any wiser to my witness account. I'm speechless, and so is Sasha. Sasha knows how important Max is to me and understands my mind regarding the clusterfuck that is my current situation.

And as the doting mother in her kicks into high gear, she starts trying to soothe my wounded heart by a redirect, talking about the new artists she's going to be showcasing in the coming months. I hear her talking, but I'm not listening to a word she's saying.

I halt in place, releasing my arm from Sasha's. She stops to turn and face me, and at that moment, I lose it. Tears fall, and I can't seem to catch my breath. I should be angry. Angry with myself for asking Max to wait for me and completely ghosting him while I sorted out my future. I should be angry that he made me a promise that he couldn't or wouldn't keep. But instead, I feel like dying.

Sasha holds me tight in her arms, tucking my head between her neck and shoulder with her hand. My chest heaves, my brain hurts, my heart breaks as she tugs me in a little tighter. We stay like this for a short time in the restaurant's back alley while I find the strength to collect myself.

I ease my body from Sasha's and run my fingers under my eyes to rid my face of the tears. "How does he know Teddy?"

"I don't know Livie, but I heard she's selling her apartment and maybe Max is her agent. We all travel in connected circles no matter how big New York seems."

I nod regardless of what the real answer to my question is. The fact of the matter is that he's moved on. I need to go home to my womb of an apartment and wallow in my sorrows. This is a turn of events that I could never have imagined.

When I return home from my lunch with Sasha I surround myself in my thick duvet cover while the Chamomile tea in my cup next to my bed grows cold without me having taken one sip of it. My mind reels, trying to analyze how I could have fallen so hard for a man incapable of being true to me.

I hurt. I hurt all over.

I thought a good night's sleep would have helped me clear my head, but Max's beautiful face confiscated my every thought when I awoke. All those tweets he posted that I somehow thought were directed discretely to me were probably not. My ego believed his impassioned, beautiful thoughts about love and life were about me. They could have been about anyone. How many other women has he dated during our hiatus? How could I have been so blind?

But now I realize that I was smart to keep him and his fake love at a distance. Maybe somewhere in my heart I knew he wasn't what he seemed, but it was so lovely to believe otherwise. Max was everything I thought I wanted in a man. He was smart, sexy, successful, said the most beautiful things to me, and I latched on to him without a second thought. I am my own worst enemy, but I've learned my lesson. I'm much stronger than I this, and as trying as my current life is, I will come out a winner as long as I stay focused on what matters to me most. And at this time in my life, it isn't love, it's my art.

I swallow a muffin and down a cup of coffee but don't bother to shower or even get out of my pajamas before I'm back to working on my sculpture. The finer details in the foam tops of the waves are all I have left to complete, and with a steady hand, I rake, loop, and hook my way through to completion. Once again, I lose myself in my work, and the hours pass like minutes. It is nearing two o'clock in the afternoon before my stomach growls at me, breaking my concentration. But it's done. My masterpiece that broke my bank account in supply costs is finally complete.

I slowly spin my potter's wheel to scan every angle of the sculpture one more time. I could fuss with the details for another two weeks and still find more to add or subtract, but that is the fault of the artist; never knowing when to stop. The next stage is to apply paint and have it fired for the high polish finish I'm after. I will use a thin underglaze to give the upper part of the wave a watercolor effect and then apply a heavier acrylic paint for the base's darker section.

For now, I'll have to wait a few days until my next alimony check arrives to my account. I've used every spare penny I have on this project. I'm financially and emotionally drained, but the end to my life's trying circumstances are near.

Chapter 34 – Max

I could have sworn I saw the back of Olivia's head exiting from the rear exit of the restaurant but, that visual makes no sense. I'm seeing things now that I've had three bourbons while dining with Teddy. The server asks if I'd like another cocktail, and I place my palm in the air and tell her no, thank you. As much as these drinks are going down smoothly and my company is entertaining, I know my limits. And it is only one-thirty in the afternoon. I have paperwork to tend to and a client meeting at three-thirty this afternoon.

I remind Teddy that I have to get back to work, and she pouts at me playfully. I chuckle at her and give her a quick kiss on the cheek as I button up my jacket. "I gave Harjit the day off to study for her pilot's license test next week. Do you mind dropping me off at the office?"

"Not at all, Max." She waves her hand gently in the air, and our server comes to our table. "The check, please," she says, and that is my queue to pull out my credit card. For a brief moment, Olivia's lovely face enters my mind again. God, how I miss her.

During the drive, I check my Twitter account to see if Olivia has posted anything, but she remains silent. It is like she's suddenly fallen off the grid, and it annoys the fuck out of me that I have no idea where she is or that she won't return my calls. Maybe she went back to Carl. Fuck. Wouldn't that be a strange twist of fate? I let out a long breath and stare out the window of Teddy's limo.

"Are you alright?"

I fake a smile and reply, "Yes." As the limo comes to a stop at the front of my office, I lean in to give Teddy another quick cheek kiss and tell her I'll connect with her later.

The following day while inside my office, I pour what is left of the coffee pot into my cup and head to my desk to hunker down for a few hours of paperwork, but just then, my cell rings. "Hello, this is Max."

"Max," Carl says. "I wonder if I could convince you to stop into my office at the University for an hour this afternoon. I want to discuss housing options around the University area now that we've got an accepted offer on the apartment."

I check my watch and glance over my desk. These papers can wait until tomorrow. "Yes, that's fine. What time works for you?" I ask.

"Four?" he offers.

"I'll have to push back my staff meeting until tomorrow morning, but that will be fine, Carl. How do I find your office?" Carl gives me directions to the University's wing and where to locate his office. I jot notes down on a scratchpad to be sure not to get lost. I realize I'll need to leave here by three o'clock to make the appointment with Carl, and I'm dreading having to drive myself anywhere now that I have Harjit as my personal driver. But, it might be a nice change to drive my car alone once in a while, and I tell Harjit to go home to do more studying.

I'm wandering down the halls of the University when I spot Olivia. I have to do a double-take as I feel like I'm having another vision instead of a moment of reality. She's here. She's fine and alive. "Olivia!" I call out down the corridor, and she stops to turn in my direction. She's forty feet ahead of me, but I can see her shocked expression even from this distance. I had hoped that her beautiful smile would grace me, but she remains unsettled by my appearance. "Olivia. How are you? Where have you been, my love?" I say as I quicken my pace to where she stands.

177

The Art of Love in New York City

"My love?" she repeats, incredulously. "I think you have me mistaken for Teddy," she says as her arms shuffle anxiously between being crossed over her chest and loose at her sides, then she plants her hands on her hips. "Never mind. I don't have time for relationships, and I'm better off without dating a cheater," she says and turns her back to me just as I'm a few feet away from her.

"Olivia. What the hell?" I ask while I try to reach her and stop her from leaving my sight.

"Max. It's over, and you know it. I can't be your leftovers or option number two. If you want to date multiple women, then you can count me out. That was never on my agenda," she huffs, then quickens her pace down the corridor toward the courtyard exit.

My heart sinks deep inside my chest. She *was* at the restaurant yesterday, saw me with Teddy, and escaped out the back exit. "Dammit, Olivia. Stop for a bloody minute and talk to me," I demand. She does as I ask as she holds the exit door open for just a brief second then leaves without turning around to see my face. I'm following her until I get a chance to explain.

Busting through the exit door and not giving a dam that I'm going to be late to meet up with Carl, I run to catch up to her in the courtyard and stop in front of her, so she has no choice but to address me. "You refused to tell me where you lived, never answered any of my phone calls or texts; explain to me how I'm supposed to interpret that, Olivia."

Her eyes lift to meet mine, and she searches them briefly. "I'm broken, beaten and tired, Max. I was focusing on the only thing I could trust – my art. I never stopped loving you or needing you during that time. I thought we agreed to let me have this space to get my life back in order, but you just couldn't keep your hands to yourself." She strokes a wayward hair from her eyes and tucks it behind her ear. "I get that. You're a man, single, free to do whatever you please. I was a stopover along the Max Donovan highway, and when the going got tough, you bailed. It isn't as surprising as I thought it would be, Max."

"Whoa, there, Olivia," I say as I place my hands gently on her shoulders. "You were not under any circumstances a stopover. I'm in love with you. Teddy came into my life when you abandoned us, and I decided that if you were no longer interested in me, then I should move on. I didn't go looking for another woman to replace you. It just happened."

Olivia's eyes begin to water, and now she's upset. "I never abandoned us, Max. I was very clear on what I was doing and why I couldn't have you with me while I worked out my personal issues. YOU made me a promise." She releases her shoulders from me with a shrug and a step back. "You said, and I quote, *I am not a patient man, but for you, I will wait.* In that statement, you didn't give me a time limit." She pauses and begins waving her arms around the front of her body, frustrated. "I took you at your word, Max, but I guess your word means nothing. Enjoy your relationship with Teddy."

I let Olivia slip past me as I look skyward and shake my head. I slowly turn around, watching her wander off to the courtyard's opposite side behind the fountain and call out, "All you had to do was return a phone call or send me a text, Olivia. That is all you needed to do for me to keep waiting for you as I promised I would. This is on you." I let out a long breath and return to the wing for my meeting with Carl. At the very least, she now knows my feeling about our agreement.

I decide that from now on, Clint can deal directly with Olivia as I can't seem to get through to her. She doesn't want to be near me. This much is clear after today's encounter. But, I need her final decision on buying Russell's loft by the end of this week.

The Art of Love in New York City

Teddy is no replacement for what Olivia is to me, and as sobering as that thought is, I've made my bed. Who knows where my fling with Teddy will lead? And do I want it to lead anywhere? I can only hope that one day Olivia will come to her senses, but the promise of that future remains dim. I'm unclear as to how hard I need to press Olivia to make her see that she is the only woman I want, that I need in my life. If I give her more time, will that fix the damage I've done or will Olivia hold that against me, against us, forever?

Chapter 35 – Olivia

Feeling relieved that I got my words out of my head and voiced to Max lifted a weight off my chest that I didn't realize was so heavy. The past twenty-four hours were the straw that broke the camel's back for me in that I had anger, emotional confusion, and stress over seeing him with Teddy, of all the women in New York, but now that has all lifted. Sometimes confronting issues head-on is the only resolution. Had I thought of this earlier, I may not have left Max alone to wonder about us as long as I did. He is right; this predicament I'm in with Max is all on me.

I will retrieve my completed wave sculpture tomorrow after it has been bisque fired. I can't sleep, wondering how it will turn out as the excitement is too much. The number of hours, money, blood, sweat, and tears I put into it all comes down to how it looks after the firing. No matter what I created in form, the color, once fired, is the crowning glory, and until it is revealed, there is no telling how happy I'll be with it. Then I'll need to add the glaze and fire it one more time.

Five days later, I get to see the sculpture double fired and ready to ship to Sasha's gallery. I haven't sent her any pictures of it since before it was painted, so I hope she is as delighted with the finished glazing as I am.

The vision I had that I sketched from four perspectives came to life far better than I had hoped. On one side, you clearly see a wave cresting, the curled tips of the wave edged in white foam. From there as you walk around it the crest begins to resemble a hand reaching out. When you step to the other side you see the second hand of the lover connecting to the first hand, and the lower wave edge resembles a flowing flamenco dress in an upward flare, which was the hardest part to incorporate into the overall sculpture. I do my slow walk around the finished piece, tracing my fingers over the surface, looking and feeling for any imperfections, my heart pounds with sheer delight. I hear the owner of the shop from across the warehouse call out to me.

"I've seen some pretty amazing sculptures come into my shop in my lifetime, but that one is special."

I cannot help but grin from ear to ear hearing his words. It is a glowing compliment from someone like Bruce. "Thank you so much. It was a huge undertaking, but I think I achieved what I had envisioned when I started it." Bruce walks over to where I'm standing and has another look at it with me.

"Have you titled it yet?"

"Yes. I'm calling it The Dance, but in Spanish. So, El Baile will be its official name."

"That's perfect. Did you plan to have it look like two people dancing? Or am I seeing something in it that wasn't intended?" he asks, now gently tapping his lip with his finger as he admires it from a different angle.

"Yes! That is exactly what I wanted to convey. I'm so glad you see it!" My enthusiasm makes Bruce smile and wink at me. "It's masterful, Olivia. You've come a long way in all the years we've been firing your sculptures."

I kiss Bruce on the cheek and give him a quick shoulder hug. His wife, Stacy, is nearby and watching us. I wave at her, and she smiles back. "He's right, Olivia. It is truly stunning. You've outdone yourself."

"I have the delivery truck coming in half an hour to transport it to the Lipinski Gallery. Can we crate it now, so they don't have to wait?" Bruce nods and signals to one of his staff to help him place my sculpture into a four foot by four foot, padded wooden crate. Bruce uses a lift system to pack larger clay pieces, and this one is heavy, coming in at close to two-hundred-fifty pounds. I grit my teeth and wince as the lift carries it off the platform, and El Baile is slowly guided by hand over to the open crate. Just as the boys are positioning it over the crate, the crane suddenly drops by six inches, and the boys scramble on their feet to hold it in place so that it doesn't drop to the concrete floor. I screamed and nearly passed out while gripping my hair in my hands at either side of my head. "NO! Jesus Christ! Are you kidding me?" My heart is trying to pound its way out of my chest as Stacy rushes over to me to try to keep me calm.

"It's fine, Olivia. See?" she says, pointing at it now stabilized and being lowered into the crate. I let out a long jagged breath and nod.

Bruce looks over to me and nervously chuckles. "That was a close one, hey?"

"I swear you did that on purpose just for a laugh," I charge, half-joking and fanning my face with my hand.

"Trust me. My heart is pumping just as hard as yours is. Sorry we scared you, Olivia."

Once it has been loaded onto the truck, I pay Bruce for his services and head out in my car to meet the delivery truck at Sasha's gallery. I'm about to climb out of my car to meet up with Sasha when I receive a text message.

Max: There's still time.

"Time for what?" I ask myself aloud. "Jesus," I say as I exit my car and lock the door. I wrestle in my head for the next half hour about his text, trying to understand what he's talking about. I don't want to engage him because he's moved on. Teddy could be a perfect match for Max. As much as I hate to admit it, I can see them being good for each other. Another text comes through from Max, and now I'm getting upset.

Max: "Is the sculpture complete?"

I figure I may as well reply to that one, so he'll stop texting me. "Yes," I type hastily. There. I'm done now.

Max: "When can I see it?"

Me: "Stop texting me. You know where to find it. Why are you so interested?"

Max: "Because I want to know what I was competing with for your time."

Me: "It wasn't a competition. Please, stop texting me."

Max: "If you still want the loft, let me know. I'll send someone over with the paperwork."

I hesitate to reply to Max about the loft apartment. It is my dream space, but living there would only remind me of Max, how beautiful he was to me, and how that seemingly perfect relationship got so messed up.

Me: "Tell Russell I'm sorry. It will only remind me of you, and I can't do that to myself. This is over, Max. I beg you to stop texting me. I'll change my phone number if you don't stop."

Max: "You once told me that I couldn't see the forest for the trees. Here's one more idiom: You are biting off your nose to spite your face, Olivia."

I stop to open the door to Sasha's gallery and read Max's last text two more times. What does this mean? Is he trying to goad me into texting with him further? Then, one more text message fills my cell phone screen.

Max: "I have all the respect in the world for you and your achievements. But there is a part of you that remains unfinished, Olivia. I know this because I, too, feel incomplete. We belong together, now more than ever. Don't let what we had end before it has the chance to be so much more."

Chapter 36 – Max

"Why does everyone call you Teddy?" My tumbler of bourbon gets swiftly replaced with a fresh glass only moments after I set the nearly empty cocktail on the table. "Thank you," I say to the server.

"It is a short version of my full name. My mother's father's name was Theodore, and when I, her only child, was not born male she decided on calling me Theodora. The nannies all called me Teddy from as far back as I can remember. Even my mother does."

"That is an interesting story. It sounds like something out of a Gone with the Wind kind of setting; Southern women drinking iced tea on the porch of a Colonial plantation house," I muse. I reach for my new cocktail on the table before adding, "Although, Theodora Braithwaite has a decidedly English ring to it."

"You find my name and stories amusing, do you? That's adorable, Max. Trust me. I may have grown up surrounded by incredible wealth, but no amount of money replaces the love of your parents or their time with you growing up. I have more respect for my nannies than I ever had for either of my parents. Daddy is trying to make up for it in his own way, and Mother is still too busy playing bridge and drinking with her friends to worry about what her adult daughter is up to. I don't care how that sounds or looks to you. Money *can* buy you happiness in certain ways, but it will not buy you love."

My jaw flexes at Teddy's sideways insult to my observations. I was making small talk, but Teddy seems to be on the defensive tonight. I apologize, and she accepts that I meant nothing by my remarks. "Can you spend the night?" she asks as she rises from the table and tucks her purse under her arm.

"Yes, of course." I stand and help Teddy on with her sweater, then follow her to her limo. Considering I've been dating Teddy for nearly a month, one would think we've had sex more than twice. While that thought pops into my head she asks me, "Have you ever had a three-way? I don't mind sharing you."

I'm stumped for words, but I manage to stay cool, calm, and collected while I formulate a reply. "Yes. But that was a long time ago in college. Is this something you do frequently?" I return my gaze out the window of the car while I wait for Teddy's reply. I can't help but chuckle as I'm beginning to think I'm the only man left in town that hasn't participated in a menage et trois since college. In these little moments when people share tidbits of their lives or personalities, you gather a bigger picture of who you are with. I would not have imagined Teddy being the sharing type in bed, but now the truth is out there.

She still hasn't answered my first question, so I ask a different one. "Are you into male, female, male or female, male, female?"

Teddy breaks out into boisterous laughter. "Either way is fine with me.

"I think most men would rather a three-way with two women." Just as I finish my statement, we arrive at Teddy's building. I follow her up to her apartment, but now I'm feeling awkward toward her. As we enter her apartment, she says, "Relax, Max. Have another drink. I just want you in my bed with me tonight. Take your clothes off and meet me in my bedroom," she says while kicking off her shoes and throwing her Fendi purse, which likely cost more than my last commission, atop the marble entry hall table.

My back gets up instantly at Teddy's command. It felt so flippant, and I can't let it slide. "Are you telling me what to do? Is this what you want? Me, kowtowing to your every whim?" My jaw ticks as I continue. "I'm not that guy, Teddy."

Teddy turns to meet my eyes as she stands in the hallway.

Her expression softens. "I'm sorry. That isn't how I meant my words to be taken. You are welcome to do as you please, Max."

Perhaps I was a bit on edge and reacted too quickly. I'm here physically, but my mind is elsewhere. I'm wondering where Olivia is, what she's doing, and why I can't make her see me the way I need her to. Grabbing the drink I'm now desperately needing, I knock it back, feeling the burn like it were a punishment. I need to make a decision about where I stand. If I continue to see Teddy, I'm only shooting myself in the foot concerning any chance with Olivia again. Tonight is my last night here.

I woke before Teddy did this morning and grabbed a bathrobe from her ensuite before wandering her apartment. Her chef has arrived and is preparing breakfast. He handed me a tall glass of fresh-squeezed orange juice, and I suddenly felt like I was in some fancy hotel. I nod and smile, raise the glass to my lips and savor the sweetness of the juice. As I pass the housekeeper, she gives me a timid smile, and I offer her a "good morning."

Teddy has an office space where her assistant spends most of her time, toiling away at who knows what. I should know what her interests are other than art collection and high-end real estate investments, but we've not discussed it. As I poke my head curiously through the office door, I notice a watercolour painting hanging on the wall adjacent to the desk. This must be a new purchase as I've not noticed it before. The longer I look at it, the more I am intrigued by it. Why does this artwork look so familiar? I step inside the office and confirm the artist's name on the bottom right corner. Olivia Aston. Of all the unexpected coincidences, Teddy has one of Olivia's watercolours.

I should be happy for Olivia to have sold another piece of her art but instead, a knot forms in my belly, and I remind myself of the question I pondered last night; what am I doing with Teddy when Olivia is the only woman I need?

The knot grows bigger, and my emotions attempt to get the best of me the longer I stare at the painting. I had always wondered what true love felt like, and now I'm in the heat of loss from the one person who taught me what true love is. I understand now when I hear people refer to it as dying inside. The expression always seemed so overdramatic, but in truth, it isn't. The image of Olivia's smile, the recall of the sound of her sweet laughter, the light in her eyes when she looked at me; those moments in our time together will never fade for as long as I live.

I clear my throat of the tickle that sits there as I'm about to turn back toward the kitchen. Just then, I feel a soft hand over my shoulder breaking my rumination and then a little kiss upon my cheek. "Breakfast is ready, Max. Come join me. You need something to eat," Teddy says. I feel her fingers slip between mine as she moves to lead me to the breakfast table. I clear my throat again and straighten my posture attempting to rid myself of my private little moment in Teddy's office.

"When did you buy the Olivia Aston painting?"

"A few weeks ago. I only decided where to hang it in the last two days. I will find a better place for it to hang in my new apartment. It's beautiful, isn't it? How are you familiar with Olivia's work?"

I swallow the last of my juice in my glass and rest the cup on the kitchen counter before sitting with Teddy at the table. "Would you like another?" the chef asks, and I nod. "Yes, thank you." As I'm handed my second glass of juice, I reply, "Olivia is a client and a friend," I offer since the truth of how my heart feels about her cannot be revealed to Teddy.

"She is lovely, isn't she? We spent the night together after a gallery event. I'd be interested in doing that again, but with you. I think you, Olivia and I could have an amazing night together," she says casually as she spreads jam over her toast.

I'm mid sip of my juice when Teddy makes her comment and I nearly choke on the liquid. A bit of juice has dribbled out of my mouth on to my housecoat and I grab my napkin to clean myself up.

"Are you alright?"

"Yes, I'm fine," I reply sharply. The juice went down the wrong side," I add, shocked at Teddy's comment and annoyed that I've spilled on myself. *Are you fucking kidding me? Olivia and Teddy? Jesus, could my world get any fucking smaller?*

"Do you have plans for this evening?" she asks. I don't, but I'm going to keep that information to myself. I'm a bit Teddy'd out at this point, and the longer the image of Teddy and Olivia together in bed fills my head, the more pissed off I become. Then the image of Kelsey kissing Olivia resurfaces, and it is all I can do not to lose my shit. I need to escape the minute breakfast is over.

The knot in my stomach returns, but this time it isn't from need, desire, or hopelessness. This time it is from deep-rooted jealousy that I had no idea was hiding inside me. Kelsey, Olivia, and Teddy have become connected in ways I can't fathom. And the woman that holds my soul hostage is dead center of it all. I'm beginning to feel like a pawn, shuffled across the board in random spaces that don't make the game any more exciting with each move. I'm not used to being or feeling out of control. Inside I'm screaming, "Fuck!" while I clean up the mess I made from choking on the orange juice.

"I should get to the office sooner than later this morning," I say. Teddy nods as she continues to eat her breakfast. "And I have a client to meet this evening before they leave town on a business trip."

Teddy nods in acceptance of my fake obligations, and I'm relieved she didn't press me further. Finally, an inch of control is back in my hands.

After breakfast, I'm swift to gather myself and my belongings and head out the door. Teddy kisses me as I leave, and I should have been more receptive to her at that moment, but my head is ready to explode. For fuck sake. How many women in New York are bi-sexual anyway?

Chapter 37 – Olivia

When I arrive at the Lipinski Gallery, Sasha is tucked away in her office, reading blogs on local artists and taking notes. She is constantly on the lookout for artists she'd like to bring to the forefront and with her clout in the art world, she is capable of taking a nobody to a somebody within weeks of her discovering them. She has always been a supporter of local artists, unlike many other gallery owners in this city.

She raises her head from her laptop and smiles sweetly at me. "Livie, why don't you have a glass of wine to calm your nerves. The delivery truck will be here shortly."

"I know. I'm just so excited for you to see the sculpture, and I'm nervous that something is going to happen to it during transport since Bruce nearly dropped it while packing it this morning."

"Are you kidding me?

No! I nearly had a heart attack." Taking in a deep breath, I realize that I do tend to get anxious easily these days. "No wine, but a cup of coffee might work." I head to the coffee room and pour myself a fresh cup. Just then, the rear door buzzer rings out, and I put the coffee mug back down and race out of the room toward the delivery entrance. "It's here, Sasha!"

I hear a little laughter come from Sasha as I run over to the overhead door and unlatch it. I roll the door up, and I feel like a little kid filled with excitement that Sasha is finally going to see my finished piece. I am proud of myself for completing this vision, but when I get validation from Sasha, it means the world to me. She's always honest with me about my craft, and her honesty has made me a better artist. The delivery truck doors open, and a man hops into the back of the truck to load the crate onto a hand truck to roll it into the delivery bay.

"It's nearly two-hundred-fifty pounds, Sasha. You're going to need a sturdy display stand for it." Sasha nods at me as she signs the documents confirming delivery while I'm busy looking around for a prybar to pop the top of the crate open. I find the prybar on the shelf next to the bay door and begin pulling the nails away at the top. Sasha stops me and takes the pry bar from my hand. "Brandon!" she calls out. "Come open this crate for me, will you?"

"Brandon? Who is Brandon?" I ask.

"He started here last week. I needed a big strong kid to deal with these kinds of deliveries and keep my loading bay organized. Sweet kid, fresh out of high school and built like a linebacker." Sasha winks at me, and I giggle. "He works in the mornings for me, then goes to a community college in the afternoons."

As Brandon unveils my sculpture, my excitement reaches its peak. Sasha pulls away at the bubble wrap around El Baile, and I watch her expression closely. I'm not disappointed. Her face lights up, and she gasps, "Livie. I'm dumbstruck. This, this is absolutely stunning!"

I am beaming with pride as she and Brandon tear away all the excess packing materials to reveal the sculpture fully. "The form is beautiful, but the way you painted it is, god, I'm lost for words, Livie. Brandon, we have to get this inside the gallery immediately. Let's place it on the round marble table in the center of the gallery and clean it up. Grab the mini-lift, and let's get it in there," Sasha instructs. She turns to me and gives me the strongest hug I've ever gotten from her. "Baby, you are going to sell this piece in no time. I'll have clients begging to have it. You just wait. The minute they see it there will be a bidding war."

Chapter 38 – Max

Beneath the surface, Russell reminded me. Dig deeper. These words echo inside my head as I think about Olivia. For fuck sakes, I think of her while I have sex with Teddy, and that has to be a sign that I'm going about my love life all wrong. If I can't get Olivia out of my head and I can't get her to see that we are perfect for each other, then I'm in a stalemate situation. Something has got to give.

My analysis of my situation gets interrupted by one of my staff with a double knock on the glass panel next to my office door. Kindra is our newest addition to the team and still a bit green, but she has a fire in her belly for this business. I tip my head up from my papers to see her standing at my office doorway.

"Are you free? I need your advice on how to price this property. Nothing in the area has sold in the past year, so there are no comparables to work with."

"Sure. Show what you're trying to price?" Kindra passes the file folder to me, and I take a good look at what she's compiled. She fidgets with her hands behind her back, rocking slightly back and forth on her heels while I review what she's trying to list.

I search our server's listing system for anything we've sold in that neighborhood in the past two years, and only two other properties come up. Neither of those listings compare to this one. I lean back in my chair and look up at her interested face. "In this situation, I'd take the sales from the area in the last five years, average them out, and add twenty-percent to represent the increase in market pricing. This is my best guess, Kindra. I know from experience that few properties in that neighborhood go for sale, so all we can do is guess. Having said that, your angle for marketing should focus on the rarity of listing availability and tout all the reasons why nobody ever wants to leave."

"Thanks, Max." Her smile lights up the room as she reaches to take the folder back from my hand.

"How did you get a listing way out there?"

"A college friend inherited the property, and she's not interested in living there. She's looking for a quick sale so she can use the money to buy an apartment in Brooklyn. I should easily get a sale and a purchase out of her. She trusts me."

"Nice. Send me your ad copy before you post it, please. And make sure the pictures you use are recent. Get Kim Mah out there to take professional shots if you have to."

With that minor issue dealt with, I go back to focusing on Olivia. I wonder if the sculpture is posted on the Lipinski website. When I log on to the site, there is a new post on the main page stating there will be an unveiling of El Baile by Olivia Aston tomorrow at one PM during her first solo exhibition. I check my schedule and make a note to block that time off so nothing gets booked. Nobody is buying that sculpture but me. I've already paid dearly for it with my heart and soul.

Chapter 39 – Olivia

The first solo exhibit and the unveiling of El Baile at Sasha's gallery tomorrow has me beside myself with excitement. This could be the day that puts my name on so many more lips of wealthy art collectors—the turning point for me and my craft. While married to Carl, it wasn't important to me to earn a living with my creations, but the tides have changed, and I cannot rely on him for security. I'm inspired and scared as shit for what my future holds.

Max continues to text me regardless of how many times I've asked him not to. I know I threatened to change my number, but it was in the heat of the moment that I said that to him.

Sasha calls me just as I'm about to head out for groceries. "Hey, Sasha. What's up?

"I wanted to let you know that I'm pricing El Baile at seventy-thousand dollars," she says.

I nearly fall over. "Sasha! Have you lost your mind?"

"No, Livie. I don't think you realize how popular you've become as of late."

"But that's insane. I was hopeful at twenty-thousand just because it's such a big piece. Are you sure about this?"

"Yes! Trust me already, will you? Teddy has been singing your praises all over town and posted a picture of the watercolour painting she bought on every one of her social media accounts. She's quite the influencer. How did you not know this?"

"Teddy?" I ask, shocked. I need to sit down. I didn't tell Sasha about Teddy and I.

"Livie! Are you still there?"

"Yes, yes, I'm still here. This is really fucked up, Sasha. I didn't tell you this because I didn't think it mattered, but when Teddy took me home to her apartment that night, we slept together. Does that shock you?"

Sasha laughs as she replies. "No. I'm quite aware of Teddy's bedroom antics. But it does surprise me that you, I don't know what the right word is here," she pauses, "Participated? "Does Max know you slept with Teddy?"

"Jesus, no!"

The long silence between us lingers while my eyes well with tears. "I have to go, Sasha." I hang up the phone and press my forehead down on the kitchen table. Sasha immediately calls me back, and I let it go to voicemail. Let me get this completely straight," I say aloud. "Max and Teddy are dating. I also slept with Teddy. Teddy is the one who is promoting me around town. I swear I don't know what's going to happen next. And if Max finds out I slept with Teddy god only knows what his reaction would be since he was so bent out of shape when Kelsey kissed me.

I understand that Max wants me back, and if I'm honest with myself, I want him more than anything. But we've ended up in a love triangle, and I have no idea how to deal with this.

I meet up with Sasha at the gallery first thing in the morning. My watercolours are hung along the milky white painted walls in order of when they were painted. My smaller sculptures are placed on pedestals throughout the floor space, and El Baile sits dead center of the galley floor atop the round marble table. It looks absolutely stunning in the spotlight. It glistens in the most perfect ways with the gradient colours from dark to light from the base to the tips of the waves. I am truly proud of this creation, and I don't know if I'll ever top it. Together, Sasha and I cloak El Baile in a silky black sheet before the exhibit begins.

By one o'clock, a small gathering of art lovers have arrived. They mingle with flutes of champagne in their hands discussing my paintings and the smaller clay sculptures on display. I don't quite understand why Sasha is doing this unveiling event for El Baile, but perhaps it is her way of adding a bit of mystery to my first solo exhibit and giving her gallery another opportunity to be talked about. She's even hired a photographer to capture the event in hopes that it will be useful for marketing purposes.

My nerves are about to get the best of me when Sasha addresses her clients, getting their attention by tapping the long, pale blue crystal pendant of her necklace on her cocktail glass. "Thank you all for coming this afternoon. As you know, Olivia Aston has become quite the name in recent months," she says as she gives me a little nudge from my shoulder to make me step forward to be recognized. I smile nervously as I'm not used to being the center of attention. "Some of you are familiar with her many works that have been showcased here at the Lipinski Gallery, while a few of you may not. Today, along with her latest watercolour paintings, we have a stunning sculpture that Olivia has been working on for quite some time." Sasha pauses to smile brightly at the group gathered around the marble table in a tight circle. I step back two paces to get out of the way when I feel a hand gently touch my shoulder.

"Olivia," Teddy says in her cool, confident voice. I turn to see her smiling at me, and she leans forward to kiss my cheek. I had to come today to see what you've done. I wouldn't miss this for the world," she adds.

I am surprised to see her here, and I'm not sure how to respond. As much as I know she and Max are an item and the thought of it makes my stomach turn, I cannot in good conscience not be kind to her, considering she's part of the reason so many people have come to my solo exhibit today. "I'm so glad you could make it," I manage to say with as much sincerity as I can muster. "Are you interested in the sculpture, another watercolour, or are you here just to support me?"

"Oh, darling. I'm your biggest fan, and my credit card is burning a hole in my purse," she says while clinking her glass to mine.

"That's very kind, Teddy." Just as I take my eyes off Teddy, I spot Max entering the gallery. I haven't seen him since our confrontation at the university, and my heart sinks a little at the realization that he's here, along with Teddy. Max is handed a flute of champagne just moments after he enters, and I watch as he scans the room while he takes his first sip. Does he see me? Does he see Teddy standing next to me?

Sasha pulls the silk cloak off the sculpture, and the room begins to fill with the sounds of clapping and comments as they soak in the full body of El Baile. My eyes widen as the visitors move around the sculpture to appreciate every angle. Within a few minutes of the unveiling, questions come my way about how I envisioned such a piece, what was my inspiration, and is it meant to convey a specific message. Then, in a soft, and incredibly sincere voice next to my ear, I hear Teddy breathe, "Olivia. This is – oh, it's magnificent. I have to have it." Teddy's hands squeeze my shoulders from behind me, and a gentle, seductive kiss is placed on my cheek. I'm not sure how to react to Teddy's words and touch or to the myriads of questions coming to me all at the same time. I address Teddy's sweet words as I turn around and kiss her back and give her a warm hug.

I've never felt more validated than I do at this moment by all this attention. Turning back to the guests, I address each one of them while Sasha looks on with an expression of pure satisfaction over this new level of success we are both having. So many small things came together; some so very unexpected.

The Art of Love in New York City

Raising my eyes over the shoulders of the people I'm chatting with, I see Max standing at a distance. I can't read his face from where I stand, but just then, Teddy slips up next to him and kisses his lips before looping her arm through his. His face remains expressionless while his eyes meet mine. Everyone around me begins to move in slow motion. I can feel my heart rate escalating in my chest, the sound of it thumping in my ears while all resonance of voices in the gallery dims to a soft white noise.

It is at this moment that I know exactly what I want. I refocus on the guests and their questions, smile brightly at them, and thank them profusely for their kind words and genuine interest.

Sasha has organized a bid form for those who are interested in buying El Baile. I've never had one of my art pieces up for bid due to multiple interests. I grapple with the idea that my sculpture will be sold today, and I'll never see it again. I'm highly possessive of it, I realize. Perhaps because it means so much to me in that it was everything I had emotionally and financially to create it. It is the very picture of me, a bit of turmoil, light reaching upward from the depths of darkness, a touch of hope and love, and the power of movement propelling me to think forward in my life. This sculpture is the tipping point of Max and me before I abandoned him.

I've made a decision that I think Sasha is going to kill me over. I excuse myself for a moment to slip up beside Sasha and whisper in her ear what I want.

"Livie, I can't do that," she replies in hushed voice while pulling my body closer to hers.

"Why not?"

"Oh, for Christ's sake. That would be both illegal and unethical. Think about what you're asking me to do, Livie," she scolds. "Are you drunk? I won't, and that's final." Sasha vigorously rubs her pendant necklace in her hand, sighs loudly and looks over the room nervously hoping nobody overheard our conversation. She's right, and I apologize for asking hoping that will soothe her.

Max and Teddy wander over toward me, and Sasha and I try to smile. It isn't like Sasha hasn't already done so much for me and my artistry, but Teddy owns my professional career as an artist by using her powerful influence recently to make me stand out above the din. Max owns my heart, my soul – he owns me. Our eyes meet, and neither of us can look anywhere else. Teddy begins to ask me questions, but I'm not really paying much attention to what she's saying. Then she utters the words I'd never thought I'd hear from her. "I believe you already know Max Donovan. I wasn't expecting him to come to the unveiling, but here he is," she coos, then sips from her flute of champagne.

"Hello again, Max," I say, with a bit of a stutter while offering my hand to shake with his. He returns a polite grin and a nod while placing his flute of champagne in his left hand. Our hands clasp in a soft grip that slowly becomes firmer.

"Hello, Olivia. How have you been?" He unlocks his left arm from Teddy's and places his drink in his right hand while casually slipping his free hand inside his trouser pocket.

I play along with the idol chit-chat game for fear of letting Teddy know that Max and I were once unabashed lovers. "I'm well, thanks for asking. How is the real estate business these days?"

Max's eyes narrow at me playfully, and a bigger grin emerges on his beautiful face. "Excellent. In fact, that loft you inquired about is still available. You should take another look. I think it's perfect for you." His eyes hold steady on mine at the not so subtle reminder of the first time we let our feelings about each other be known.

"Yes, it is perfect. I'll have to talk with you later about it if that's alright."

"Yes, of course."

Teddy has been playing ping pong with her eyes as each of us speaks. "What do you think, Max," she asks out of the blue.

"About what, Teddy?"

"About, you know, getting together. The three of us like I suggested." A Cheshire cat grin forms over Teddy's blood-red painted lips, followed by a giggle before she takes a sip from her glass. I get the feeling she's also not trying to be so subtle.

Max clears his throat. "We should talk about that later." Teddy winks at him and takes another sip from her flute.

In an attempt to change the subject, I turn my attention back to Sasha, who seems rather enthralled in our discussion. "What is the deadline for the silent bidding?"

"Bidders have until nine PM tonight to submit, and those who could not attend will bid online," she replies coolly without taking her eyes off Max. I hear the sound of Sasha subconsciously react by tapping her champagne flute lightly three times with the large ring on her finger while who knows what thoughts are going through her head.

I nod and try to think of something else to say, but my nervous energy hijacks my attempts to remain calm. "Excuse me." I slip past everyone to exit the gallery and collect myself in the open air. What did Teddy mean about the three of us? I should have clarified if she meant dinner or lunch. But at the moment, I can't decide which is more pressing on my emotions; the thought of never seeing El Baile again or seeing Max's arm wrapped around Teddy's. I knock back the balance of the expensive bubbly in my flute in hopes it will provide the courage to be stronger but I know I'm only fooling myself.

While I pace the sidewalk in my own little world of worry, I hear the gallery door open, and I glance up to see who is leaving. "Olivia," Max calls out to me.

I keep my back turned as I reply since I don't want him to see my expression of dread. "I can't talk to you now, Max. Please," I say. I turn to face him and hold up my hand to stop him. "It is killing me to see you in there with Teddy's arm wrapped around yours. I know what I gave up, but I don't care to be so blatantly reminded of it. Not tonight, of all nights."

"Olivia," he says again while slowly approaching me at the edge of the crumbling sidewalk curb. I square my shoulders and hold my head high. "I need to talk to you. How, after all this time, do you not have any idea how deep my love for you goes?"

I laugh at the shock of his words, and my smile conveys my incredulous feelings. I wag a finger in front of him. "No, Max. I don't. To my understanding, your love goes as deep as the next woman who makes a pass at you."

Max's expression turns dark and disapproving of my words. "That isn't fair Olivia, and you know it. We talked about this. You abandoned me and wouldn't even tell me where you lived for fuck's sake." I watch as he tries not to lose his cool, but it is too late for that. "How the hell am I supposed to interpret that kind of move from you? And, if I'm reading the room correctly," he says, now dangerously close to where I've stood my ground, "You are not so happy with the results."

I gulp hard at his words, knowing he speaks the truth. The ugly truth. His face is inches from mine, his stance is firm, hands at his sides, and shoulders rigid as he leans in. I know I'm not going to make matters better, but I say what is on my mind, regardless. "Did you come here to create chaos for me or to bid on El Baile?"

His jaw ticks before he affirms, "To see you and to bid on it. I know you created it for me. It's mine, and I don't care what it costs, but it's coming home with me." (be calmly assertive here, annunciating clearly and slowly to make a point).

I laugh again, not just at myself but at Max's intuitive understanding of what El Baile means to both of us. He sees me clearer than I see myself sometimes. "Do you know that the bidding starts at seventy-thousand?"

"Yes. I'll pay anything for it, Olivia. Anything."

"Is that the price of your love?"

"Dammit, Olivia." Max grabs my arm and pulls me in tight to his chest. I'm in shock at his swift movements but within seconds I am limp in his embrace. His lips touch mine with the same hunger he had for me in the loft. He refuses to give up on me, and I believe he is regretful for his affair with Teddy. I try one more time to escape him, but he only squeezes me tighter. "No," he states with full conviction. Max's hands cup my face now, his forehead resting against mine, his eyes glassed over on the verge of tears when he whispers, "You are not getting away from me this time, my love."

My lips tremble at his bold stance, but I let his lips kiss mine, and I hold him close while my heart bleeds out all over this empty sidewalk. He stops kissing me to say, "Don't ever shut me out again." Max grips my chin firmly, not holding back his deepest emotions, then devours my mouth again with his intense passion.

When we finally stop kissing and remain still, holding each other, his lips pressing against my forehead, I tell him my newest secret. "I, um, I may have asked Sasha that no matter what the bids were that you were the one who was to own El Baile. She struck me down on that but..."

Max chuckles with his lips still pressed upon my forehead. "Did you now? And why on earth would you think it smart to turn down the highest bidder for whatever I was willing to offer?"

"Because it was inspired by you, by who we were, what was possible between us before I went off the deep end. I don't want anyone else to have it, and I didn't realize that until people started filling out bidding forms."

"Oh, baby," he says, chuckling lightly at me. "You have no idea how happy that makes me. *Almost* as much as you letting me hold you and kiss you again."

"Are you laughing at me or the situation?" I ask, knowing he's likely laughing at both.

Just then, the door to the gallery opens up again, and both of us tip our heads in the direction of the gallery to see who's leaving. Teddy clears her throat but remains her elegant calm self regardless of what she's seeing. "It appears I may have been outbid," she states while quirking her right eyebrow high.

Max and I relax our embrace. I muss with my hair and pretend to straighten out my dress as Teddy moves forward. As she devours the distance between us in her long sultry stride, head held high, a half-filled champagne glass still within the grip of her hand, she gently presses Max's shoulder away, and he allows her a face to face with me.

Teddy stares into my eyes, and I get the feeling I'm going to be ripped a new hole for kissing her lover. Instead, she tips her head down just a hint, pours the balance of her champagne into my empty flute and kisses me passionately.

This is as unexpected as it is sensual, and I'm temporarily hypnotized by her gesture. "You and I belong together, Olivia," she whispers over my lips after they slowly part from mine. Her hand grazes the tender skin of my exposed cleavage as her smile forms while she admires me. Her eyes follow upward from my heaving chest to my lips. She pushes a wayward strand of hair across my forehead and continues to speak in her whispered voice. "We can both play with Max, but at the end of the day, all I really want is you. Don't you see that?"

I'm stunned by her admission. I slowly shake my head once while her words sink into the muddied waters of my brain. Teddy takes my flute from my hand and places both hers and mine on the ground at our feet. And before I can respond to her question, she adds to her plea for my affections. "I put you on the lips of an elite list of art collectors because I adore you and your artwork. I can buy you a life you could only imagine, Olivia. Don't deny we have something truly amazing between us. Please. Come home with me tonight."

Teddy's eyes search mine while the back of her hand still tenderly rubs the skin of my chest. Her eyes hood as she leans in to kiss me again. I let her have this moment. Her spell and those plump red lips remind me of how beautiful she was to me, but she isn't Max and could never be Max.

It takes everything I have in my heart and soul not to want to disappoint her, but I must. I'm certain of what I need and want now more than ever. I clasp her hands in mine and choose my words carefully. "You are an amazing woman, Teddy." My back straightens while I take in a strengthening breath. I am conflicted emotionally. My eyes dart swiftly to Max, then back to Teddy. I don't want to hurt her, because her affections have meant so much to me, but I have to be honest and firm.

"I adore you and all you've done for me, but I'm in love with Max. We've known each other for quite some time, but we parted ways a few months back. In the time since I let him go to sort out my upended life and to create El Baile, he found you. I was devastated when I discovered you and Max were dating. But I was willing to accept that the better woman won, regardless of you not knowing I even knew Max let alone was in love with him.

Teddy steps back from me but doesn't let her hands slip from mine. "Max and I need to go back to where we were and start again. I never stopped loving Max during my hiatus."

Teddy's eyes search mine while my words register in her head. I think she thought Max was making a move on me and that this connection was brand new. I stammer a bit before I continue. "You...you hold my career and my immense appreciation in your hands, Teddy, while Max, well...he holds my heart."

I pause there while I wait to see how Teddy reacts to my confession. Her brows knit tight, she lets out a long, jagged breath and squeezes my hands tight in hers. "I'll admit I didn't expect that." A quick, nervous smile flashes at me, but when it fades, her eyes narrow. She twists her head to look squarely at Max, then returns her gaze to me. Her eyes soften the longer she looks into my eyes. "I rarely lose, Olivia, but I have to respect your honesty." Teddy releases her hands from mine and steps back a pace. She turns to look at Max again and says, "Once again, the truth bites me in the ass. As I've said before, money can buy happiness in certain ways, but it cannot buy true love."

As she slowly slips away from us, heading back inside the gallery, she says one last thing. Her hand tentatively holds the handle of the door when she turns to say, "Olivia. If you ever change your mind, you know how to find me."

Chapter 40 – Max

We waited inside the gallery until the nine o'clock deadline to see who the highest bidder for Olivia's sculpture was, and not surprisingly, regardless of me bidding as high as I could go, I wasn't the proud new owner of El Baile. As it turns out, Teddy provided the highest bid, and the sculpture that belongs in my hands is in hers. After our encounter outside the gallery tonight, it feels incredibly ironic. But deep down, I knew I could never have outbid Teddy.

With Olivia back in my arms, it seems moot to have not won the bid on the sculpture. All I really wanted was her, but I feared that was no longer possible, until tonight. Perhaps, one day, Olivia will create another similar, smaller wave piece specifically for me.

Exhausted from the stresses of today, Olivia begged me to let her go home to her tiny apartment alone, and with much hesitation, I finally agreed. She promised that she and I would celebrate her successful solo exhibition tomorrow night, and spend the day and night together, uninterrupted by anything. It is rare for me to take a day off, but for her, I'll do anything.

It took some swift handiwork from my secretary and myself to organize the perfect date with Olivia. I think she's going to love what I have planned, and I'm anxious for her to see what I've arranged for dinner that I feel like I'm going to burst. I calm myself by focusing on having her hand in mine, walking through the city streets, and talking about what our ideas of the future could be.

All of our past indiscretions, misunderstandings, and bad

judgments during our separation are gone. We agreed to begin again with a fresh slate, starting our relationship on new ground. As our stroll across the Brooklyn Bridge nears the end, my excitement grows. I call an Uber to pick us up at the Cadman Plaza, but I don't tell Olivia where we're going.

It isn't until we take the corner to Hicks Street that Olivia's smile comes my way. "Are we going to the loft?"

"I have a special surprise, or two, or three there for you." I squeeze her hand in mine as she gives me one of her giggles and a finger tucked under her nose. God, I love it when she does this.

We exit the Uber and ride the private elevator to the loft space. Before the elevator door opens, I grip her hand in mine again and ask her, "Are you ready?"

She nods and smiles brightly at me. The elevator door opens, and I watch Olivia's expression closely. Her eyes light up and she laughs heartily. "Max! This is so romantic!"

"I know. I did good, right?"

We step out of the elevator and Olivia does a full once over of the space with her eyes. In the center of the loft, a small table is dressed in fine china, tall candles and wine glasses that I purchased from a store downtown. There is a chef-prepared meal that I ordered for us that my secretary picked up and delivered on my behalf. The loft is filled with the aroma of fine spices of a braised beef main course and assorted sauteed veggies.

I lead Olivia to the table and pull the chair out for her like a gentleman. I quickly serve her a savory celery soup as a starter with warmed sourdough bread. Olivia is devouring her dinner and knocking back the wine like it were the first meal she's had all week. This makes me smile as I only want her to be happy. So far, so good.

The Art of Love in New York City

When she finishes her last bite of the roast beef, she sips from her wine glass and places her elbows on the table, nesting her chin in her palms. Her eyes fix on me, and a slow, sexy as hell smile comes my way. "What is surprise number two, Max," she asks. Her eyes flash wide at me, and I'm instantly hard for her.

"Surprise number two is to tell you that you can have this loft, if you are still interested, now or whenever you are ready. No rush. And the price is still the same as it was when I got Russell to lower it down for you."

"Well, isn't that exciting! How were you so sure that I'd still be interested in buying the loft?"

I fold my left arm over my right on the edge of the table and lean forward to address Olivia's question. "I wasn't. But what I did was buy the loft from Russell as an investment in case you chose not to take it off his hands. This way, I could guarantee you'd get it if you still wanted it, and Russell could be off the hook waiting for a sale. I'm much smarter than I look, you know."

"That you are, Max," she says sweetly. Olivia's eyes lock on mine, and we stare at each other for a long moment. There's a sorbet dessert in the fridge when you are ready."

Olivia excuses herself for a minute to go to the washroom, and I take a moment to add a little ambiance to the bedroom as part of surprise number three.

One of the bonuses of this loft that I'd forgotten to mention to Olivia is that it is wired for full stereo sound in each room. When she returns from the bathroom, I rise from the table and open the cupboard where the stereo components are hidden. "Would you like a little music to dance to?"

"Yes," she says as she joins me in the middle of the open space. "I chose something completely cheezie, too classic for words and I know you're gonna love it," I say assuredly. She smiles as I give her a little spin with my hand around her waist. "Are you ready, Ms. Olivia Aston?"

"Yes," she whispers as her lips pull in dangerously close to mine. I steal a kiss, click the remote button in my hand, and the first notes of Billy Joel's New York State of Mind begins. Olivia's laughter fills the cavernous space, and I can't help but laugh with her. I shrug and smile before I mention, "It seemed like a good idea at the time."

"It's perfect, Max. I do love Billy Joel, and we are in New York."

"Well, Brooklyn technically. So glad you approve. Win number two," I say as I pull her in close for a slow dance. We cover only a small space on the floor while we dance, but I don't mind. I'd rather hold her close, hear her soft breaths in my ear, have her warm, beautiful body tight against mine. I don't really deserve her, but I'd never admit that. It's my secret that I'll take to my grave. As the song nears its end, Olivia tips her head up to catch my eyes in hers.

"What was surprise number three?"

I continue to dance with her even after the song ends, knowing another slow number is right behind. "Surprise number three is just down to the left around the corner behind the kitchen."

"Isn't that where the bedroom is?"

"I think so. I can't honestly remember. Shall we go have a look?" I ask, pretending to have no clue. Olivia quirks a brow and lets me lead her to the bedroom. As I slowly press the door open, she sees what I've prepared for us.

"Wow," she says as she fans her face. "Max, that is so beautiful."

The Art of Love in New York City
"Are the candles too much?"

"You're kidding me, right? The candles are the perfect touch. You sneaky, sneaky man. I'll bet you thought that if you wined and dined me that you'd get lucky too, hey?"

"It's on every red-blooded man's date menu. It's called manssert and we guys pay handsomely on date nights in the hopes of getting some." I can't believe how I pulled that sentence off with a straight face. Deservedly, Olivia punches me in my shoulder but then laughs at me.

"Alright. Manssert it is. Show me how this works," she teases as she slowly walks over to the tastefully fitted mattress with satin sheets and a plush white duvet on the floor surrounded by a variety of lit candles. "Do I lie here, or here," she asks, trying to make fun of me.

"Oh, baby. You serve yourself up any way you want, and I'll eat. Just let me get you naked first."

My plan was not complicated. Since the day Olivia sent me the video of what her facial and vocal reactions were to pleasuring herself with a sex toy, I've been dying to see her do it again in front of me. I can only hope she is game to my plan, and the only way to find out is to ask.

At the side of the mattress on the left is a black velvet bag with a drawstring tie. As Olivia lies upon the mattress on her back, propped up on her elbows, I wriggle my eyebrows at her playfully, then lean down to collect the bag.

"What have you got there, Max?"

"Are you interested to know what is inside my little bag of tricks?" I swing the bag slowly in front of her eyes and pray she nods, says yes, or giggles. Either way, I'll get the answer I need. She licks her lips and nods.

"Fuck, yes."

I kneel before her, spread her legs apart and slide up close to her. While leaning down over her to take a kiss from her plump, moistened lips, I use my free hand to undo her blouse buttons. Her desire for me is in every ounce of the kiss, and my cock grows harder by the second.

Releasing her from her blouse, I taste the warm skin around her neck, slowly following the shape of her form toward her supple, full breasts. She tips her head back while I slip the straps of her black bra over her shoulders and pull the bra cups down to expose a part of her that I adore. "God, you are so beautiful."

Olivia uses her hands behind her back to release the bra, and I dive in at the opportunity to play with her nipples with my tongue and my teeth. She seems to enjoy my little bites and tugs, and I love to see how long I can make her nipples peak from my teasing. "What are the toys that you brought?" she asks as her head tilts back up to watch me indulge in her silky skin with my tongue.

"Two different vibrators, a water-based lube, and a massage oil," I say between kisses over her belly. "But you get so easily wet for me I don't think I'll need the lube." (add a chuckle here, please)

"Hmmm, true," she moans, "But if you want to fuck my tits, I think the lube will come in handy."

"Hmmm, true," I say, mimicking her. "I swear the scent of you is an aphrodisiac. Do you have any idea what you do for me?"

"I have a faint idea," she says, smiling like a fool, and she giggles. I begin to undress, tossing my clothes left and right of where I stand. Olivia removes her jeans and white lace panties, and now we are both completely bare to each other. "Tell me all about it, Max, but wait until I have your cock in my mouth. I want all the dirty

213

details while I wrap my tongue and lips around you."

"Jesus, woman. Are you trying to make me blow my load before I even get near that sweet pussy of yours?"

She laughs heartily at me, and I follow suit. But I wasn't lying. She has that much control over me, and I don't think she realizes it. My greedy mouth finds her as wet as I'd hoped as I slip my tongue between the engorged folds of her sex. Her breaths hitch as my tongue circles her clit, and I take a few gentle sucks on it to test her response. My cock could not be any harder than it is now. I feel the need to stroke myself while I lick and suck at her pussy and decide I'd rather she stroke or suck me off while I pleasure her.

Repositioning myself with my throbbing cock over her mouth and my lips eager to taste her pussy again, we greedily get what we need from each other at the same time. She is wickedly good at fellatio —too good, and I'm ready to come too quickly. Her lips and hot mouth sucking at my head while her hand squeezes and strokes my shaft is pure fucking heaven. As I near the point of no return, my mouth devours her, and I suck at her clit, wanting desperately for her to come at the same time as I do. The intensity sends us off the precipice of glory in near unison and in spectacular fashion. I swear this woman was made for me.

I quickly turn myself around and hover over her, face to face, diving onto her mouth to kiss her hard while we both labor to catch our breath. "You are so delicious, Babe. Fuck, me, you are so good. I don't deserve you."

As I roll to her side, we continue to hold each other close, our lips and tongues still tangling together. My chest hurts – a sensation I've never felt while making love with a woman. This is strangely incredible to me that my love for her actually makes my chest ache. "What are you doing to me?" I murmur over her swollen pout. Olivia's hands gently cup the sides of my face while I stare deep into her soul. Her eyes glisten in the simple candlelight, and a single tear slips slowly over her cheek. She senses it too. Nothing feels more real than this. Nothing else matters but her.

"I love you, Max," she whispers, and that ache in my chest gets stronger.

We relax for a while like this, forehead to forehead, eyes closed, softly breathing and sharing intermittent tender kisses.

"How was your manssert?" she asks, finally breaking our silence.

"Amazing. The best I've ever had. Speaking of dessert, can I offer you a bowl of sorbet from the fridge?"

"Yes, please."

I rise to my feet from our cuddle to retrieve the sorbet bowls prepared by the chef from the freezer and two spoons from the dinner table. We enjoy the soft, ice-cold peach flavored concoction in record time while my mind conjures up ways to implement the sex toys with her. "Are you ready for round two, Babe?" I ask and wriggle my eyebrows at her again.

"Is that the bat signal for *I want to fuck you senseless*? Should I look for that little eyebrow wiggle as my clue?" she asks in a sultry tone. Her hand reaches for mine, then she begins to teasingly suck slowly at the tips of my fingers, one by one making me rock hard for her again.

Setting aside our dessert dishes, I reach for the bag and pull out a small hand vibrator and place it in the palm of her hand. "I need you to show me how you pleasure yourself like you did in the video you sent me. I want to watch you indulge, hear your moans, and those little high-pitched squeaks of pleasure when you're almost ready to come. Will you do that for me?"

The Art of Love in New York City

I get a little head nod and a bright smile. "That's my girl." Olivia takes the vibrator and turns it on. She lays back on the mattress, smiles sweetly at me, and places it between her legs moving it up and down over her sex, spreading her natural wetness over herself. She begins to focus on the bit of flesh just above her clit, and my eyes widen at the beauty of the scene unfolding before me. This is so hot. My own little perfect porn star masturbating in front of me.

Instinctively I fist myself and begin to stroke slowly while I watch her face relax, and I listen for her breathing pace to increase the longer she circles her clit with the toy. I'm entranced by watching her become more and more aroused. She squeezes her breast and rolls her nipple between her fingers while the vibrating toy in her other hand fulfills her need and mine. My fist instinctively grips harder and pumps over my shaft a little faster.

"Ah, ah, ah, ah, ah," she chants in hot-as-fuck breathy hitches. Then I hear that sweet sound of her little whimper just before she releases, see her eyes roll back into her head, eyelids fluttering, her hips rising just seconds before she crashes through her orgasm. I'm so involved in watching her while I'm stroking myself that it only takes a few moments longer before I explode over my hand. She watches me as I ease my grip and pump myself a few more times, completely emptying myself.

I don't miss the opportunity to lap at her swollen pussy with my hungry tongue and taste the bounty she wrung from herself for me. "That was amazing. I could watch you do that all day long."

"You're welcome, lover. It was good for me too," she says, licking her pretty lips.

I have yet to allow myself to sink inside of her, and I'm not letting this evening end without that need fulfilled. We take another brief break to lay beside each other. The ache in my chest has subsided as it has been replaced with a high like no other. I try to break our heady silence as we rest with a question. "So, have I sold you on this place yet?"

Olivia busts out into a fit of laughter while my smart-ass grin beams back at her. When her laughter begins to subside a bit, she says, "I don't know, Max. I think I may need to Christen it one more time before I can make any firm decisions." And with that, we are both rolling on the mattress in unstoppable laughter.

Epilogue – Olivia

I'm still in a bit of shock at the fact that twenty-eight of my thirty watercolours on display at my solo exhibit have been sold, along with Teddy's winning bid on El Baile. My bank account brims with profits, and my confidence has soared to new heights.

I wander around my new space with the last box to unpack held in my tired arms. Max has been busy at the office, finalizing the sale of Teddy's apartment. He managed to get a bidding war happening, and it sold for two-hundred thousand over asking. The success of that deal will bring Max many more like it with Teddy as his champion supporter.

Max and I had lunch last week with Teddy and explained our story to her. She graciously accepted our decline of her offer and admitted that when she saw us outside of the gallery during the solo exhibit, she knew she'd lost me to Max.

I'm beaming inside with joy from having taken over possession of the loft from Max. We've become inseparable in the past month since my exhibit. He spends every available minute with me, but I don't mind it one bit. And I must admit that this loft really is *our place* and it was the moment he showed it to me so many months ago.

As I rest the box on the kitchen table and open it to discover what it holds, I find inside, of all bloody things, my marriage certificate to Carl from nineteen years ago. For a brief moment, it makes me sad as I brush my fingers across the paper document. The good news is that Carl has settled into his new residence just four blocks from the university grounds, and he seems content. With that realization coming to the forefront, I slip the document back inside the manila envelope and carry it over to the recycling bin. We've moved on and in good ways – both of us much happier than when we were together after his stroke.

My cell phone buzzes from atop the kitchen counter, and I see that it is Max checking in on me. "Hello, lover."

"Hi, Babe. I'll be there in twenty minutes. Is there anything you need me to pick up for you?"

"No. I've got everything I need," I say, and my heart literally smiles at the utterance of that sentence. Nothing could be truer.

"Good to know. See you soon."

When Max arrives home, he waltzes out of the elevator with a huge bouquet of mixed flowers in every color of the rainbow for me, I rush toward to greet him. "What are the flowers for?"

"Their beauty cannot compare to yours, but I thought they'd act as a welcoming present now that you've finally gotten all your boxes unpacked."

"I love them, Max. Thank you." As I stroll over to the kitchen, I slip in a little question that has been burning in my mind. "And when are you moving in?" I ask as casually as I can while placing the flowers inside a tall glass vase.

"What did you say?"

I pause my arranging of the flowers and smile at him. "Move in with me. We're together ninety percent of the time, Max." I fuss a bit with the arrangement of the flowers again while I wait to see how he'll react to my question. I'm hoping I'm not making him nervous. I stop touching the blooms and peek over them to catch Max's eyes fixed on me. "What?" I ask nonchalantly.

Max approaches me to wrap his arms around my waist from behind me then whispers in my ear. "Your serious?"

The Art of Love in New York City
"Yes."

A warm kiss is placed on my cheek. "Is right now too soon?"

"Right now is perfect."

The End.

About the Author:

Sandra was born in Vancouver, British Columbia, Canada. Her artistic nature led to an avid interest in art and photography from an early age, and that passion continues today. Her foray into the realm of writing romance novels started as a personal challenge to write a romantic made-for-television movie script in her spare time, but instead it became her first full-length novel.

Sandra was nominated for a Society of Voice Arts and Sciences award (SOVAS) in 2024 for her audiobook production of The Irishman's Promise for which she wrote, cast, directed, and engineered. Sandra is also a proud member of The Writers' Union of Canada.

<u>Additional Titles by This Author:</u>

Avalon

Rain on a Tin Roof

The Playboy Next Door

The Voice From 808 – One Wrong Number Changes
Everything

The Creative Director – The Heart Never Lies

The Art of Love in New York City

From Bridges to Breakdowns – Not all Rock Legends Are
Members of a Band

The Companion

Tempted: The Erotica Anthology

The Irishman's Promise

Wild Orchids

Website: www.sandrasigfusson.com

www.ingramcontent.com/pod-product-compliance
Lightning Source LLC
Chambersburg PA
CBHW031959240626
47153CB00003B/1034